Sweet Secrets in Pennsylvania

D1557429

To Carol aka Gracie

—C.P.E.

For Tricky Ricky

—C.L.W.

Published by Familius LLC, www.familius.com
Familius books are available at special discounts for bulk purchas-
es for sales promotions, family or corporate use. Special editions,
including personalized covers, excerpts of existing books, or books
with corporate logos, can be created in large quantities for special
needs. For more information, contact Premium Sales at
559-876-2170 or email specialmarkets@familius.com.

Library of Congress Catalog-in-Publication Data

2013940130

ISBN 978-1-938301-76-6

Printed in the United States of America

Edited by Preston Wittwer and Aven Rose
Cover and book design by David Miles

10 9 8 7 6 5 4 3 2 1

First Edition

Sweet Secrets in Pennsylvania

CHERI PRAY EARL AND
CAROL LYNCH WILLIAMS

ILLUSTRATIONS BY MANELLE OLIPHANT

MEET THE
STOCKTON FAMILY

Matthew
Stockton

Grandpa
Stockton

Laura
Stockton

Gracie   George

AND KEEP YOUR
EYES PEELED
FOR...

Crowe

Milton
Hershey

TRACK THE ADVENTURE

Delaware

Pennsylvania

It Happened Like This . . . I Swear

I'm George. And my sister's name is Gracie.

Gracie is nine years old. So am I.

We're twins, but I'm older than she is by 5.75 minutes.

She's taller than me by one and a half inches.

But I'm smarter by about two feet.

Gracie and I live with our grandpa. He's a fix-it man. He works at the Stockton Museum of Just About Everything in American History. Our family's museum.

Mom and Dad used to work here, too.

Except we haven't seen them for two years. Since they found the time machine.

That's when our trouble started.

Mom and Dad used the time machine to travel back in history. They bought really great stuff for our museum. Then they got trapped in time. We never know where they are. Or where they are going to be. Or when.

We sure miss them. A lot.

Me and Gracie have a plan to get our parents back. We have to return all the stuff they bought for the Stockton Museum. Then Mom and Dad can come home.

The problem is, now we have to ride in the time machine.

And we have another big problem. Mr. Crowe.

He's stuck in time, too. He's following us.

He wants us to take him to his time in 1879. In our time machine.

But if we take him home before we return everything, before we rescue our parents . . . we might never see Mom or Dad again.

And then we might get trapped in time, too.

CHAPTER 1

Off and Runny

"Aa-choo," said Gracie. "Excuse me."

I took off my glasses and wiped them on my shirt. "Could you aim that spit at somebody else, please?"

"Can I help it if I'm allergic to you, George?" Gracie said. She smiled at me.

A huge map of the United States was pinned on the fix-it-shop wall. Me and Gracie and Grandpa watched a little red light flash on the map. Right over Hershey, Pennsylvania.

"Gracie, look," I said. I pointed. "That must be where we're going next."

"Mom and Dad are there," said Gracie. "Waiting for us." She touched her locket. The one Mom gave her.

The big wall clock said it was after midnight. That's late for me and Gracie. But we wouldn't be here long. I mean, here in Grandpa's fix-it shop way in the back of our family's museum. The Stockton Museum of Just About Everything in American History.

We're taking off to rescue our parents. In the time machine.

Taptap tap tap taptap tap tap went the old telegraph.

"Sh-h-h-h, kids," Grandpa said. "Your parents are sending another message."

He sat down at the old telegraph machine. Me and Gracie ran and stood next to him.

Mom and Dad. My stomach got all jittery.

Gracie squeezed my hand.

We watched Grandpa write down the message.

"Pennsylvania . . . 1903."

"Let's go," I said. I pushed up my glasses with one finger. "We know where they are, so what are we hanging around here for?"

"You're not going anywhere," Grandpa said. He

pulled two sandwiches and a small bag of potato chips out of a brown paper bag.

"Not until you eat these," he said. He handed the sandwiches and chips to me and Gracie. "Who knows how long you'll go without food once you get to Hershey."

Gracie patted Grandpa's arm. "Don't worry, Grandpa," she said. "We know what we're doing."

I tried to eat my sandwich, but I didn't feel hungry. I was afraid to travel back in time again. Swirling in a time machine is scary. My stomach gets tied in knots. My hands sweat. My eyes go all wet. I couldn't tell Gracie, though.

Because she's braver than me.

That's the way I see it, anyway. Of course, I'll never tell *her* that. It would go straight to her head.

We *had* to go back in time to save Mom and Dad. Even if I was scared to go. They were still out there somewhere. Trapped in the past. And only Gracie and I could bring them home.

Grandpa paged through a tall stack of papers next to the telegraph machine. "According to this, your mom and dad bought a rug from a Mr. Milton Hershey in Hershey, Pennsylvania. In 1903."

"Hershey?" I said. "Like the candy bar?" This trip

was sounding better now.

Gracie rolled her eyes. "1903?" she said. "Ick. That means I'll have to wear a dress when we get there."

"I'll bring in the rug while you kids eat," Grandpa said. He left the room.

I took a bite of my sandwich. Tuna and pickles. My second favorite. I like tuna and chips best.

"Hey, Gracie. Maybe you'll get lucky and turn into a llama this time," I said. "Or an iguana. Then you can't wear a dress."

When we traveled back in time to Delaware, Gracie turned into a horse. Now *that* was funny.

Gracie put her hands on her hips. "Grow up, George," she said. "This is serious."

I crossed my eyes at her.

"Besides," she said. And then she raised one eyebrow. "Maybe you'll be the iguana this time."

"Gulp," was all I could say back. Because I hadn't thought of that. "Gulp gulp."

Grandpa came back in the room. He dragged a rug behind him. A big red one with gold fringe on the edges.

"Whoa!" I said.

"It's huge," said Gracie.

"And heavy," said Grandpa. He dropped the rug on the floor in front of us. Dust puffed into the air. "But it's beautiful, isn't it? Too bad we can't keep it for the museum."

Gracie knelt down and stroked the rug. She sneezed again. "Mom and Dad touched this," she said.

"How will we ever get that in the time machine?" I said.

"It will fit," said Grandpa. "You'll see." He took a deep breath. "I should be the one to go back in time," he said. "Instead of you kids. It's downright dangerous, the two of you going alone like this."

"But you can't go, Grandpa," I said. "You've been to the past too many times already. With Mom and Dad. And you brought stuff back, like they did."

"So you could get trapped, too," Gracie said. "And then what would happen to me and George?" She touched her locket again.

"Yes, yes," said Grandpa. "I know." He looked tired.

"We'll be okay, Grandpa," I said.

I said it. But I wasn't so sure.

Crowe would be waiting for us when we landed in Pennsylvania.

For us and the time machine.

Grandpa told us not to trust Crowe. Mom and Dad warned us about him, too.

Gracie held Grandpa's hand. She was scared, too. I could tell by her face.

Then she turned to me. "Okay, George," she said. She took a deep breath. "Let's go."

I walked over to the corner where the time machine had landed after our last trip to Delaware in 1776. The time machine always changes shape when it travels. It was an outhouse in Delaware. Now it was an old trunk.

I ran my hands over the trunk. It jiggled and sort of purred. "Yep," I said. "It's awake."

The time machine seems to like me and Gracie. I guess that's a good thing.

"Why does the time machine change shape when it travels?" Gracie said. She got her scrunched-up thinking face on. It's not pretty to look at, I tell you.

"I'm not sure," said Grandpa. "But I have a theory. I think it's trying to disguise itself."

"Crowe can't steal the time machine if he doesn't know what it looks like. Right?"

"That's what I think, George," Grandpa said.

"See, Gracie?" I said. I tapped my forehead. "I

keep telling you. I am the brains of the family."

Gracie snorted.

"Pay attention to what the time machine changes into when you get to Pennsylvania," Grandpa said. "You can't get back home if you can't find it. And if Crowe gets to the time machine before you do . . ."

I felt my stomach squish up. "We'll be trapped in time, too. With Crowe."

"You can't let that happen," said Grandpa. He put his hand on my shoulder. "Remember, Crowe has to go wherever the time machine goes. And he knows who you two are now. So take care of each other."

"We will," Gracie said. She squeezed her lips together, tight.

We all got quiet. Grandpa's worried face told me that in another minute, he wouldn't let us go. But we *had* to. Even if we were scared.

"Come on, George," Gracie said. "Let's put the rug in the trunk."

I tried to smile. "Okay, Gracie."

Gracie's got guts. That's for sure. Brave guts.

Me and Gracie pulled on the rug. We could hardly move it. Grandpa helped.

When we got the rug close to the trunk, the

trunk shook and made a strange humming sound.

The lid flew open and WHOOSH! The rug disappeared inside.

I fell back into Grandpa.

Gracie fell into me.

"Cool," I said.

"That's so dangerous," said Gracie. "If we got our fingers caught in there . . ."

Grandpa shook his head. "All these years traveling with the time machine and it still surprises me," he said.

"I guess it's our turn now," Gracie said. "Ready, George?"

I wanted to say, *No way. I'm* not *going.* But I didn't.

"Yeah," I said.

Grandpa hugged us both.

"I wish you didn't have to go," he said. "Do not forget that Crowe will be waiting for you."

"Don't worry," I said. "We know who he is now. We'll be careful."

Gracie nodded. "I'll take care of George," she said. She put her arm around me. "You know how he is."

"Yeah," I said. "Brilliant."

Grandpa smiled.

Gracie climbed into the trunk. It grew wider.

I climbed in after her. The trunk got even wider.
Like a mouth.

"Ouch! You're on my ankle," Gracie said.

"Sorry," I said. I sat down and crossed my legs.

Grandpa stood back.

"This is it, Gracie," I said.

She rubbed her ankle. "I've done this before, you
know," she said.

The time machine made a loud whirring sound,
like a helicopter, and lit up. Two pairs of seatbelts
grew out of the sides of the trunk and snapped together over our laps.

My heart flip-flopped.

Gracie clutched her locket.

We stared at each other.

The whirring sound got louder and louder.

The lid on the trunk started to close.

"Be careful," Grandpa yelled.

I nodded. So did Gracie.

She reached over and took my hand.

"We'll be okay, George," she said.

Then BANG! The lid slammed shut.

And ZOOM! We were inside a black hole.

CHAPTER 2

You Dirty Rat

The time machine stopped whirring. It thumped to a halt.

I looked for my hands. "No," I said out loud. "Please let me have people fingers."

I turned into a horse in Delware. Guess what I had then? That's right. Hooves.

There wasn't much light here in this old trunk. If we were even in the trunk still. Something smelled funny. Like dried grass. And old milk. And . . . *ick* . . . poop.

I touched my face. Girl hands. Whew! At least I wasn't a llama.

"Mooo."

"George?" I said. "Oh no."

I couldn't see George. But I could hear him.

"This is not good," I said. "This is not good at all, George."

"What?" George said.

I touched my necklace. For sure I had fingers. It's always a good sign when a girl travels through time and ends up with fingers.

But poor George. Poor, poor George.

"You're a . . ." I said.

"Mooo," George said.

" . . . a cow," I said.

"What?" Now George's voice was high and squeaky.

"What's wrong with your voice?" I said. "A minute ago you were mooing at me. Now you're squeaking."

"What are you babbling about?" George said. "I'm not mooing. Er . . . at least, I don't think I am. *Eeep!*"

"Where are we?" I said. "I can't see a thing. And I have got to check and see if you're a Jersey cow or a Guernsey."

I waved my hands around where George's face

would have been.

"I can't see Gracie," George said.

"You never could see," I said. "Did you drop your glasses?"

"No," said George. "I can feel them on my face. But boy, can I hear. It's like I have super hero ears. I can even hear you flapping your arms around. And it sounds like you're wearing . . . oh too bad. You're wearing a dress. And with your luck, it's an ugly, weird dress."

"Mooo."

"I didn't know cows had such good ears," I said.

I felt around on my legs. Blast. There it was—the dress. Winding around my knees.

"I'm telling you, Gracie," George said. "I'm not a cow."

"Then why do I smell cow poop?" I said.

"*Eeep!*"

"What's that sound, George?" I said.

"What do you mean? *Eeep!*"

"There it is again," I said. "Something said, '*Eeep!*'"

"Hey. I have the super hearing. If something said '*Eeep!*', I would hear it. Let's get out of this trunk and get the rug back to where it belongs. I want to find Mom and Dad and go home."

The sooner everything was back where it belonged, the sooner Mom and Dad would be home. Where *they* belonged.

"I don't think the time machine is a trunk anymore, George," I said. I patted around. My fingers found something cold and made out of metal. "This feels like a handle."

"Grab the handle, Gracie," George said. "See if it goes to a door out of here."

I turned the cold metal handle and pushed the door open.

"It is a door," I said. "But something is covering it. Like a blanket."

"Push through," said George. "I'll get the rug. *Eeep!*"

"Do you have the hiccups, George?" I said.

I took a step forward. Next thing I knew, I was on the ground.

"Pthewy." I spit hay out of my mouth. I could see! I got up and brushed myself off. I had fallen out of a car. I think. It was covered with a thick black blanket. All that showed were the wheels.

I looked down at my dress. I held it out a little. George was right. It was weird. But I kind of liked it.

Except for the apron part. And the button-up boots. But I liked the chocolate color of the dress. And the little rosebuds

I heard giggling behind me. From inside the car. Then George said, "Are you okay, Gracie?"

"I think so," I said.

"Nice boots," he said. He giggled some more.

"Be quiet, George," I said. "I'd rather wear a dress than have one hundred stomachs. And hiccups that won't stop."

"Mooo."

The sound made me jump. Right beside me was a live cow. Live *cows*. Five of them.

We were for sure in a barn.

Bright light came into the barn through two doors. Maybe a hundred more cows were outside. Or a thousand.

Even though it was stinky, this place was pretty tidy.

There were neat stacks of hay. Big brown bags full of seeds. Pitchforks, shovels, and lots of other tools hung on one wall.

"I smell corn," George said. "*Eeep!* Smells good. Sweet."

"Quit thinking about food," I said. "We have

work to do."

I turned back to the time machine, which was now a car.

George and I would have to be careful leaving the barn. Crowe was probably somewhere close. Watching for us. Watching for the time machine.

"Can you give me a hand, please?" George said. "I can't even budge this carpet. It must have gotten a lot heavier when we traveled through time."

I turned around. I pulled the blanket off the door.

The time machine looked like a mini stagecoach with bicycle wheels. Giant bicycle wheels. The windows were covered with black shades. So *that's* why it was so dark inside that thing. The name *Hershey* was painted on the side.

I glanced at George and the rug inside the time machine.

And froze.

Like an ice cube. A popsicle. No, an icicle.

"What?" George said. "Why are you looking at me like that?"

His glasses perched on the end of his tiny nose. His hair was brown and shiny. His paws curled up under his chin.

I tried to say something, but I couldn't. My lips

moved. But no sound came out.

"Mooo," said one of the cows.

"George?" I said.

George jerked a small furry paw over his shoulder like he was pointing.

"I need help, Gracie," he said. "This carpet is way too heavy for me to move alone. *Eeep!* We have to get it into Mr. Hershey's house. Hurry up before somebody catches us in here."

I took a step forward.

George craned his neck back and looked up at me. He wiggled his little nose.

"Oh no, Gracie," he said. He slapped a paw to his forehead. "You've been changed again. You're a giant this time. I mean, you are *huge*. You have got to be a hundred feet tall."

I closed my eyes for a second. Then I opened them and looked at George. My used-to-be-twin brother.

"Rat," was the only word I could say.

"Hey. You don't have to call me names," said George. "It's not my fault you're so big."

"I'm not . . . " I said.

George cut me off.

"Crowe will be able to pick you out of a crowd

for sure. *Eeep!*"

"I think he'll see you first, actually," I said.

"At least *you* can get the rug with no problem. Pick it up between your fingers like a carrot." He paused. "Mmmm, carrots. I'd love a carrot right about now. *Eeep!*"

"Stop talking about carrots and listen to me," I said. "You turned into a rat."

George wiggled his nose.

He touched his glasses.

He held his paws together like he was praying.

He turned.

A long gray tail stretched out behind him.

"I'm a *rodent*?" he said.

Then George fell over in a dead rat faint.

CHAPTER 3

Driving Miss Gracie

"George," Gracie said. "George, wake up."

I opened my eyes. I stared up Gracie's big fat nose.

"*Eeep!* Don't breathe in, Gracie," I said. "You'll suck me up like a vacuum cleaner."

"Stop kidding around, George," she said. She poked me in the gut.

I sat straight up on my little rat's tail. "*Eeep!*" I said. I touched my nose and my mouth. And my . . . "I have *whiskers?*"

Gracie giggled. She covered her mouth. "Sorry," she said.

"Yeah, I'll bet," I said.

"At least you're not an iguana," Gracie said. Then she gave me a big grin. "Notice that I'm a *girl* this time."

"Okay, smarty pants," I said. "So you're a girl. And I'm a rat. How are we going to get this rug out of here? Hmm?"

Gracie's grin disappeared.

We were in a pickle. And not a sweet pickle, either. Yum. Sweet pickles. Wait! No time to think of food. We had to get the rug to Mr. Hershey before we could go home. But we couldn't lift it without Grandpa's help.

Then BOING! An idea bounced into my brain. Being a rat made me even smarter, I think.

I tried to tell Gracie my idea, but all that came out was, "*Eeep!*"

"Hold your breath for a whole minute," said Gracie. She pinched my nose. "Maybe that will stop the *Eep*-ing."

"Quit it," I said. I pushed her fingers away. "I told you, I don't have hiccups."

CRASH! Something or somebody kicked a bucket near us.

Gracie jumped into the car. "What was that?"

she said. She pulled the door almost shut. A line of light fell across the rug and me.

"*Eeep!*" was all I could say. But it was louder this time.

"Keep your pants on, George," Gracie said. Her voice was a whisper. "I'll check it out."

"You think I can get pants on over this?" I wiggled my tail at her.

"Don't do that to me ever again, George," Gracie said. "I mean it."

Gracie lifted the dark shade that covered the car window and peeked out. "I don't see anyone," she said. "Maybe one of the cows knocked over a milk bucket."

"Maybe," I said. But I wasn't so sure.

My whiskers twitched. And twitched. And twitched.

I couldn't help it. This rat thing was weird.

"I can't move this carpet by myself. And you're too small to help, George," Gracie said. "We need a plan."

"Don't worry. I've got one." I poked the car seat. "We're going to drive the rug to Mr. Hershey's house."

Gracie raised her eyebrows. "I hope you're

talking about the *cows* driving." She pointed her finger right in my face. "Because I don't have my driver's license. And neither do you."

Gracie is big on rules.

"Plus you're too short to reach the pedal. And the steering wheel. I'm not going to jail for driving without a license. She crossed her arms. "You'll have to think of a better plan, that's all."

I pointed a claw at her. "Do you have another idea?" I said.

Gracie stared at me with her mouth hanging open. Big as a cave.

"I didn't think so. So we have to drive the rug to Mr. Hershey's house. Wherever that is."

Gracie looked around the barn. Like one of the cows might drive.

I tapped my foot.

She looked back at me. "Oh, all right," she said. "But we have another big problem. I don't know how to drive. "

"I do," I said. "Sort of. Grandpa showed me. In that tiny red clown car at the museum. It has two seats and a gas pedal and brakes and everything."

"Sort of?" said Gracie. Her voice got higher than mine. "Do you know how to drive or not?"

"Ummm, yes," I said. "All you have to do is climb up behind the driving stick thingy."

"Then what?" Gracie said.

I talked real fast. "I'll sit up on your head. And I'll tell you what to do. It will be easy."

Gracie covered her head with her hands. "You're not putting your rat bottom on my hair," she said. "That's disgusting." Then she pretended to gag.

I nibbled on my paws. I don't know why. My rat body was out of control. And a little itchy.

"Come on, Gracie. For Mom and Dad," I said.

Gracie looked me in the eyes. Then she took a deep breath. "Okay. For Mom and Dad."

She opened the car door and glanced around the barn.

"All clear . . . I hope," she said. "Climb on."

I scrambled onto Gracie's shoulder.

"Your nails are tickling me," Gracie said. "And you better watch it with that—

My tail slapped her in the eye.

"—tail," Gracie said. She blinked.

"Sorry," I said. "It kind of keeps me steady." I wrapped it around her neck like a hug.

"I am not going to think about this at all," Gracie said. "Not thinking, not thinking . . . " She shivered.

The cows lifted their heads. They stopped chewing and stared at us.

"Mooo," one said.

"*Eeep!*" I said.

"Sh-h-h," Gracie said in her I'm-not-kidding voice. "All of you."

The cows backed off. I think they were afraid of Gracie.

Gracie stepped out of the car. She climbed up to the driver's seat. It was high on top of the car. At the back.

I held onto her collar with my sharp claws.

"Okay, George," Gracie said. "I'm ready."

I climbed up Gracie's hair.

"Ouch! Stop crawling around, George. You're giving me the creeps," she said. "This is so gross."

"I still can't see over the steering wheel, Gracie," I said. "Try kneeling on the seat."

Gracie kneeled.

"I can see, I can see," I said. I clapped my paws together. They made a *click, click* sound. "Okay, let's go. Try moving that lever."

"Which lever, George? I see two."

"The left one," I said. I didn't say, "I think." That would make Gracie crazy.

She pushed the lever. The car made a quiet buzzing sound. Then it rolled forward.

"George, the car is moving," Gracie said. Her voice was high again. "What do I do now?"

"Ummm . . . " I wasn't so sure.

"George!"

"Push the lever some more," I said. "Push it all the way."

So she did. The car moved faster.

"We're heading straight for the cows!" she said.

"*Eeep!*" I said. I almost fell off Gracie's head. I held onto a handful of her hair.

"Stop pulling my hair," she said. She slapped at me. I dodged her hand.

The cows bumped into each other and conked heads.

"How do we turn this thing?" Gracie said.

"Move the driving stick to the right," I said.

The car turned away from the cows.

"Mooo," the cows said. They looked nervous. I didn't blame them.

"Oh my gosh, George. That worked." Gracie laughed in a kind of crazy-sounding way.

"Are you okay?" I said. I bent down to see her face. Her eyes were wild. The way a cat looks in a bathtub.

"This is cool," she said. She pushed the lever again. The car moved faster.

She steered the car out the barn door. Right into the sunlight. We zigzagged around the pasture.

"I wonder where the brake is," I said.

The cows watched us go faster and faster. They probably knew where the brake was. But they weren't talking.

"Yahoo!" Gracie said. She leaned forward. "I was born to drive. I'm a natural." Then she said, "Look, a house." She pointed with her free hand.

The car swerved.

"*Eeep!*" I said. I slid down toward Gracie's ear.

Across the cow pasture stood a tall brick house. It was painted blue and had lots of windows.

By now we were going kind of fast. Heading right for the house.

Every bump made me slide off Gracie's head. So I wrapped her hair around my paw. And hung on.

Gracie kept driving. "Whee," she yelled. "This is fun."

We whizzed past bushes and scared a horse grazing in the field.

A little dog barked at us and ran away.

"You're scaring the livestock, Gracie," I said. "And that includes me."

We sped past a man standing behind a tall oak tree. He wore brown pants and a dark blue shirt. His hat was pulled down over his eyes. I couldn't see his face.

My whiskers twitched. And twitched.

"Hey," I said. "Did you see that guy, Gracie?"

She glanced over at him.

The man raised his head. He looked right at me. I saw his gray eyes. Like a cat's eyes. And his blacker-than-black hair.

"Oh, no," Gracie said. "It's Crowe. He's found us already."

Crowe's mouth dropped open when we passed him in the car. "What in the world . . . ?" he said. He stared at me. Then he saw Gracie and smiled.

"Make us go faster, Gracie," I said. I wrapped my paws tighter in her hair. "He's following us," I said.

Gracie let out a little squeal. She pushed the lever. "This is as fast as we can go," she said.

Crowe trotted behind us. Then he ran.

My little rat heart pounded. "Faster, Gracie. Faster!"

"I can't," said Gracie. She leaned forward.

"Please, car. Please."

She tried to steer toward the house. But something went wrong. Instead of going straight, the car drove around in circles.

I slipped off Gracie's head and dangled right in front of her eyes.

"Go straight, Gracie," I said.

"Get back up there," Gracie said. "I can't see, George." The car swerved to the right. I scrambled onto Gracie's shoulder.

"*Eeep!*" I said. I glanced behind us.

Crowe was close enough to touch the back of the car.

"*Eeep!*" I said again.

Crowe took hold of the side of the car. He pulled himself up next to Gracie.

The car shook and shuddered. Grandpa was right. The time machine doesn't like Crowe.

"Hello Gracie," Crowe said. "And George, I presume."

He smelled like soap. Peppermint soap.

"Leave us alone," Gracie said. "We're not helping you."

"Oh, but you are. And now we're all taking a little trip," Crowe said. He put his hands over

Gracie's hands. He made her push the lever sideways.

The car made a loud humming sound.

"We're going back to *my* time," Crowe said. "You'll fit in nicely in 1879."

"Gracie," I said. "The time machine. It's going to take us back to Crowe's home."

"Help, George!" Gracie said.

"Let me drive," Crowe said. He tried to push Gracie over on the seat.

The car jerked to the left.

I clung to Gracie's shoulder.

"Let go," Gracie yelled. She pushed at Crowe.

The car jerked all on its own, hard.

I scrambled up Gracie's hair, then flew into Crowe's face.

We were nose to nose.

"Being a rat suits you, George," Crowe said. I could tell by his voice he was mad.

I bared my teeth at him and . . . chomped down hard on his nose. Then I dropped to the floor and ran close to Gracie's feet. Right near the hem of her dress.

"Aaaahh . . . " Crowe yelled. Gracie made a sharp left and Crowe fell out of the car.

The lights on the time machine went dark. It stopped shaking.

"That was close," Gracie said. She blinked fast. Like maybe she wanted to cry. She took in a deep breath. "Good job, George."

"Thank you," I said. I clacked my teeth together. Then I climbed up onto the seat. I peered out to where Crowe was. He still lay on the ground. His hand covered his nose.

Gracie drove in circles. So we weren't too far from the barn yet.

"Point the car at the farmhouse," I said.

"I'm trying," she said. "The lever is stuck."

"It's going to be okay," I said.

Gracie's voice went low, almost a whisper. "Thanks George," she said.

"You're welcome." I blew a hot rat breath right in her ear.

"Stop it," she said.

Three men ran out from behind the barn. One carried a pitch fork. A few more men came from the house.

When they saw me and Gracie in the car, they stopped in their tracks. One big guy hollered and headed toward us. Fast.

Crowe got up from where he fell and limped away.

Now all the men chased the car around and around. Like in an old timey movie.

"Get out of that car, Miss," the big guy said. "Now."

"I can't stop this thing," Gracie said.

But somehow she pushed the lever the right way. We headed toward the blue farmhouse.

The men followed.

The big guy jogged right next to Gracie.

"What are you doing in this car, Miss?" he said.

"Driving," Gracie said. "It's my first time." She sounded proud.

A man and a woman came out onto the porch of the house. The man had a mustache. He wore overalls and boots that went all the way up to his waist. The woman wore a long pink skirt and a fancy white shirt. Her curly hair was piled on top of her head. She covered her mouth with both hands

"Who's that driving my machine?" the man called. "Sid?"

"I've got them, Mr. Hershey," said Sid.

"Did you hear that?" I said. I looked at Gracie. "That's Mr. Hershey."

"I heard," she said. She steered the car toward him.

"Are you sure this is a good idea?" I said.

Gracie leaned into the wheel. She kept driving forward.

Mrs. Hershey screamed. "A rat!" she said.

Mr. Hershey put his arm around her waist. They both stepped back.

"Go inside, Kitty," Mr. Hershey said.

"We're going too fast," Gracie said, "Hold on, George."

Then CRASH! The car ran smack into a fence and stopped.

I flew off Gracie's head.

"Eeee—yaaaag," I said.

I was one dead rat.

CHAPTER 4

All Cracked Up

George sailed right through the air when we hit the fence. Like a bird. A hairy bird. With no wings and a long tail.

Mr. Hershey snatched George out of the air like he was a baseball.

I bumped off the seat and onto the floor of the car.

"I told you I didn't know how to drive," I called to George. I wiped my hands on my dress.

George sat up in Mr. Hershey's hands. George's glasses were crooked. His tail was crooked. He twitched his whiskers at me.

Mrs. Hershey ran down the steps to the car.

"Are you hurt?" she said. She touched my shoulder.

All the men ran up to where the car stopped. I couldn't see Crowe anywhere. Maybe he was gone.

"She might be a spy," Sid said. "Move away from her, Mrs. Hershey."

Mrs. Hershey looked me right in the eye.

"This is no spy, Sid," Mrs. Hershey said. "She's a sweet little girl."

I heard George snicker. The rat.

"You know how the other candy companies are, Mrs. Hershey," Sid said. "They'd do anything to get Mr. Hershey's milk chocolate recipe. We can't trust anyone. Even a little girl."

"P-shaw," Mrs. Hershey said. "Sid, you know no one can outsmart my brilliant husband." She glanced toward Mr. Hershey on the porch. I did, too.

Mr. Hershey held George in his hand. He smiled at his wife, then came down the stairs to where we were.

George waved at me.

"This car's not going anywhere," said a bald guy in dirty jeans. His hands had grease on them. "She's banged up pretty good."

Mr. Hershey scowled. "Darn it all," he said. "Can you fix her, Elmo?"

"We can try. But I'm not making any promises," Elmo said. "At any rate, it'll take a few days."

"Sid, hitch a horse up to this contraption," Mr. Hershey said. He shook his head. "Let's take her to the shop in Lancaster."

"Yes, Mr. Hershey," said Sid. He headed for the barn.

Oh no. How would we get home if the time machine was taken away? Where in the world was Lancaster?

"George?" I said.

George smacked his head with his paw. "*Eeep!*" was all he said.

"Oh, now," Mrs. Hershey said. "We won't worry about that silly car."

"Silly car?" said Mr. Hershey. "Why Kitty. You know it's the only one in town." He ran his hand along the bent metal.

"It's a thing, Milton," said Mrs. Hershey. She turned to me. "What's your name, sweetie?"

I smiled up at her. Mrs. Hershey was pretty. Her voice was soft. She reminded me of . . . Mom. I glanced over to where Mr. Hershey's men checked out the time machine.

"I'm Gracie," I said. A lump came up into my throat. I missed Mom.

I nodded toward George. "And that ugly rodent is my twin brother, George."

But George wasn't in Mr. Hershey's hand any more. George had crawled up the man's arm. Now he sat on Mr. Hershey's shoulder.

Mr. Hershey had a strange look on his face. He said, "This rat is your twin brother, young lady? You two don't look alike. Where's your tail?"

He laughed at his own joke.

"*Eeep!*" said George. He showed two long, front rat teeth at me.

He and Mr. Hershey were a lot alike.

George laughs at his own jokes, too.

"That's not funny, Milton. I think the child has bumped her head," Mrs. Hershey said. "She's delirious." Then she whispered, "Ignore him, Gracie. He's harmless. We're going to have to get you out of Mr. Hershey's machine, though. The men are anxious to pull it into Lancaster." She reached her hand out to help me.

My heart thumped.

"Where's Lancaster?" I said.

She touched my forehead. "It's the next town over. Not far. How is your neck?" she said. "Does anything hurt anywhere?"

"No ma'am." I shook my head and tried to crawl out of the car.

But I couldn't. My dress got in the way.

Mrs. Hershey wrapped her arms around my waist. She tried to lift me.

"Wait, Kitty," Mr. Hershey said.

He moved from the front of the car to where we were. "Don't pick her up," he said.

George clung to Mr. Hershey's hair.

Mrs. Hershey put me down. "He's always fussing," she said.

"You are much too weak to do that, Kitty," Mr. Hershey said. "Come on, young lady."

He helped me out of the car.

"Thanks," I said.

"We've got to take care of our Kitty," Mr. Hershey said.

"Oh Milton." Mrs. Hershey patted her husband on the arm.

Mr. Hershey kissed her cheek.

Sid came back with a horse. "This way, Nellie,"

he said. He tugged on Nellie's harness. But she pulled away from him and came right to me. She looked me in the eye. Then Nellie nodded.

I looked at George.

George looked at me.

"Hello, Nellie," I said. I petted her nose.

"Come on, girl," Sid said.

Nellie nuzzled my cheek.

"She likes the girl," Mr. Hershey said. "Nellie doesn't like anyone."

I whispered in her ear. "You'd better go now. You know I was a horse once, don't you?"

Nellie nodded.

"You'd better go now."

She nodded again and went over to Sid.

"Did you see that, Milton?" Mrs. Hershey said.

"I did," Mr. Hershey said. "This little girl has a way with animals."

George puffed his cheeks at me.

Sid hooked Nellie to the time machine.

George looked at me from Mr. Hershey's shoulder and pointed.

"What?" I said.

"I didn't say anything," said Mr. Hershey.

"I was talking to George," I said.

Sid frowned.

Did he still think I was a chocolate spy?

Mr. Hershey turned to Mrs. Hershey. "We'd better get a doctor for this little girl," he said.

"Gracie," Mrs. Hershey said. "Where are you from?"

I blinked.

How could I say the future? It was like something from the movies. And I wasn't even sure if there were movies in 1903.

George stood on his hind legs. He waved his paws in the air.

I reached over and took him from Milton Hershey's shoulder.

"What do you want?" I said. I wanted to give him a pinch. But I didn't.

George ran up my arm and perched on my shoulder. He put his nose right into my ear.

Everyone stared at us. I felt like a rat trainer at the circus.

"The rug, Gracie," George said, real soft. "Tell them about the rug."

"Oh, I forgot," I said. I turned to Mr. and Mrs. Hershey. "We have something for you."

"And what would that be?" Mr. Hershey said.

He held out his hand and George crawled straight into it. Mr. Hershey stroked George's rat hair. If George were a cat he would have purred.

I guess the two of them were best friends now.

"Teacher's pet," I said.

George plugged his ears with his paws and pretended not to hear.

"It's in the car," I said. I shot a worried glance at George. "How will we find it again?"

George shrugged and shook his head.

"Find what, dear?" said Mrs. Hershey.

Just then, one of the men said "Giddy-up." Nellie pulled the car forward.

"Hold on there," said Mr. Hershey. The man held the horse's reins.

I motioned for everyone to follow me.

I opened the car door.

Mrs. Hershey looked inside. "Oh," she said. "That's my old rug."

Sid and Mr. Hershey dragged the rug out of the car.

"Okay," said Sid. He motioned to the man holding Nellie.

And he led Nellie away.

Pulling our time machine with her.

"*Eeep!*" said George.

"You can say that again," I said.

"How did you get this?" Mr. Hershey said. "We sold it only last week to that fellow from . . . what was the name of his museum, Kitty? Something about American History."

For the second time that day, I froze. I was an icicle all over again.

"The Stockton Museum of Just About Everything in American History?" I said.

"Yes, that was it," said Mrs. Hershey. "You've heard of it? I remember that the man had the most beautiful white poodle. Wasn't that a beautiful dog, Milton?"

Mr. Hershey nodded. "The pink ribbons in its hair were a bit much, I thought."

"What . . . what were their names?" I said.

"Names?" Mr. Hershey said. He tapped his chin like it might help him think. "Hmm. Let's see."

"The dog's name was Laura," Mrs. Hershey said. "An unusual name for a poodle."

"Right," Mr. Hershey said. "And the man—his name was Matthew."

"Glu-urp," said George.

I thought I would fall over in a dead rat faint. And I wasn't even a rat.

CHAPTER 5

Sweet Secrets

Mrs. Hershey tucked Gracie in bed in the guest bedroom. She brought her chocolate pudding. She sat in a chair beside her and watched her eat.

"Thank you, Mrs. Hershey," Gracie said.

Mrs. Hershey's face said, "You're welcome, Gracie."

My face said, "Gracie Stockton, you're a big faker. And you're eating all the chocolate pudding."

Gracie's face said, "Heh, heh, heh, George."

I stood on the nightstand. I licked my lips. I wiggled my nose with chocolate joy.

I watched Gracie gulp down fat spoonfuls of

pudding. She acted like she was the only hungry one around.

My stomach growled. I ran across the blanket to Gracie. "Piglet," I said in her ear. "Save me some."

"Rats can't eat chocolate," Gracie said. She licked the spoon. "It's like poison to them. So in a way I'm saving your life."

"No. Dogs can't eat chocolate," I said. "Rats can eat anything. Even metal. Besides, I'm not actually a rat."

"Oh. My mistake," said Gracie. She swallowed the last of the pudding.

She grinned at me with her chocolate mustache.

"She seems fine, Kitty," Mr. Hershey said. "Except that she keeps talking to the rat."

He looked at me. Then he looked at Gracie.

"I'd rather be safe than sorry," said Mrs. Hershey. "Let's hear what Dr. Oliver has to say."

She checked the watch pinned to her blouse. "Where in the world is Dr. Oliver?"

"We'll find out," Mr. Hershey said. "On our way to my laboratory. I'm taking George the Rat there with me."

I perked right up. Really? Cool.

Mrs. Hershey looked surprised. "Should you

take a rat in a place with food?" she said.

Mr. Hershey patted my head.

"I have a strange feeling," Mr. Hershey said, "that this is an unusual rat."

I nodded at Gracie.

"He sure is, Mr. Hershey," Gracie said. "He's more like a boy dressed up like a rat. And shrunk down to the size of a rat. And really hairy."

"Like a rat," Mrs. Hershey said.

"Exactly," Gracie said.

They both laughed.

Mr. Hershey scooped me up.

"We men have got to stick together," he said.

"*Eeep!*" I said. He slipped me into his jacket pocket. The pocket was deep and warm. It smelled sweet. Like candy.

I peeked out of Mr. Hershey's pocket.

I waved to Gracie. But I didn't say a word. I couldn't let Mr. Hershey know I talked. At least not yet.

"Tell the rat goodbye," Mrs. Hershey said.

"Goodbye George," Gracie said. "Keep your eye out for the you-know-what and for you-know-who."

The you-know-who was Crowe. What was I supposed to do if I found him? And the you-know-what was gone. On it's way to Lancaster. Not much I could do about that.

"You know what to do if you find them, right?" she said.

I shook my head because I did not.

"Who is she talking to?" said Mr. Hershey.

"The rat," said Mrs. Hershey.

Gracie made like she was driving.

I lifted my paws in question.

Gracie jumped up and ran in place on the bed.

I shook my head. Even *I* thought she was crazy after that.

Mr. and Mrs. Hershey watched.

"Milton," Mrs. Hershey said. Her voice trembled. "I'm worried about her."

"Drive IT . . . pick me up . . . don't let Crowe see," Gracie said. Then she coughed.

"See, Milton. She's ill." Mrs. Hershey put her hand to Gracie's forehead. "She's babbling."

I gave Gracie a claws up.

"Settle into my pocket now, George," Mr. Hershey said. "We've got some important work to check on. And a doctor to find. As soon as possible."

I snuggled down on top of Mr. Hershey' handkerchief. Yum! It smelled like sugar and dried milk.

So I tasted it. And tasted it. Mmmm.

Mr. Hershey clomped down the stairs in his big work boots. I bounced up and down and held on tight.

Mr. Hershey talked to me as he walked. "I really need to get back to my laboratory," he said. "We're so close to discovering the right mixture of sugar and milk now."

I tried to say, "Okay." But my brain was too jiggly. Plus, I didn't know what he was talking about.

We met Dr. Oliver at the front door. He was a short man with a ring of white hair. He wore wire rim glasses that looked like mine. And a suit that didn't look a thing like rat hair. Plus he smelled like cough medicine.

I held Mr. Hershey's handkerchief to my nose.

"The little girl is upstairs," Mr. Hershey told the doctor. "I don't think she's hurt. But she keeps talking to this rat." He motioned to me. "Says he's her brother. Kitty is worried about the child."

Doctor Oliver peered at me over his glasses.

I pushed my own glasses up and stared back at him.

He squinted. "Is that true?" he said. "Are you her brother?"

I showed him my two front teeth.

I said, "*Eeep!*" Then I gave a little nod.

But I stayed quiet.

A doctor might want to experiment on a talking rat.

"Hrrumpf," said Dr. Oliver.

He looked at Mr. Hershey. "Not much of a talker, is he?" They both laughed like crazy.

"Will you tell Kitty I hope to be back for dinner?" Mr. Hershey said. "She expects me. But I hate to stay away from the laboratory too long. I think we're getting close to figuring this one out."

"Congratulations, Milton." Dr. Oliver slapped

Mr. Hershey on the shoulder. I bounced in the pocket. "You'll be richer than a king." He walked in the house. "I'll tell Kitty you'll be home in time."

Mr. Hershey stepped outside onto the porch. I could smell the fields now.

"Are you hungry, George? Do you like chocolate?" he said.

Hungry? *How about starving*? I sucked loud on his sugar-milk handkerchief.

Mr. Hershey smiled. "Sounds like somebody's tummy is empty. We'll see what we can find."

We walked across the yard toward a long white building with no windows. It looked kind of like our garage at home. But bigger. And it only had one door.

The sun was setting.

Just then my whiskers twitched.

I peeked out over Mr. Hershey's pocket. But I didn't see anyone.

My whiskers wouldn't stop twitching.

We were being followed.

Crowe, I thought. *He's back.*

I crossed my claws. I hoped he hadn't discovered where the men took the time machine.

Two men stood in front of the door of the white

building. One was Sid.

A hand-painted sign on the door said, "No Admittance."

The two men moved aside for Mr. Hershey.

"Evening, Mr. Hershey," one of them said. He took off his hat.

Mr. Hershey nodded. "Charley. Sid."

He pulled a key from his pocket and unlocked the door. "Found anything out yet?" he said.

"Nope," said Charley. "But don't you worry, Mr. Hershey. Sid here's got a special gift for spotting spies."

He jerked his thumb at the other man. "Nobody will creep around here without us seeing."

Sid didn't take his eyes off me. He had a dark, angry face. It looked worse in the evening than it did in the day. Scarier.

I slipped down inside Mr. Hershey's pocket. Then I peeked out.

Sid still stared at me.

He gave me the creeps. "*Eeep!*" I said. But real quiet.

Mr. Hershey and I went inside and walked upstairs. He unlocked another door.

"We've had quite a few problems with spies,

George," he said. "It seems they want my secret recipe for milk chocolate. Sad thing is, I haven't even figured it out yet."

I said, "*Eeep! Eeep!*" Which means "I can't believe you're talking to a rat."

"Welcome to my laboratory, George," said Mr. Hershey.

I looked around.

Wow. Mr. Hershey's Secret Milk Chocolate Laboratory.

CHAPTER 6

I Spy a Spy

"So, you are Gracie," Dr. Oliver said. He set his black bag on the bed beside me.

I nodded. "Yup," I said.

Dr. Oliver reminded me a lot of my doctor back home.

Short, round, and bald. Except for a little bit of white hair.

He looked in my eyes.

He looked in my throat.

He listened to me breathe.

"I'm fine," I said. "I promise."

"Mmm hmm," he said.

Dr. Oliver looked off over the top of my head as he worked.

He checked my pulse.

He rubbed his hands down my neck.

He felt my head all over.

Then he looked back at Mrs. Hershey.

"Kitty," he said. "This girl is fit as a fiddle. I can't find a thing wrong with her."

"Are you sure?" Mrs. Hershey said. She wrung her hands. "I would hate to think she got hurt in Milton's old machine."

Dr. Oliver got a grumpy look on his face.

"You are *not* responsible for the child crawling in that machine," Dr. Oliver said. "Her parents are to blame for that. Letting a young lady like this run wild and drive cars. And carry *rats* around. Rats are filthy."

I giggled. I'd have to tell George that one.

Dr. Oliver shook his head and took off his stethoscope.

"Where are the child's parents?" he said. "I'd like a word with them."

"I don't know," Mrs. Hershey said. "We haven't gotten to that."

They both looked at me.

"My parents?" I said. I bit my lower lip. I couldn't tell them the truth.

"I . . . don't know," I said.

At least I wasn't lying. I *didn't* know where Dad and Mom were. I did know what they were. A man and a white poodle with pink ribbons on her ears.

Nobody said a word.

A bird landed outside the bedroom window. It chirped.

I tried to change the subject.

"Hi bird," I said. I smiled at the bird. Then I smiled at Mrs. Hershey and Dr. Oliver.

Dr. Oliver pulled Mrs. Hershey off a ways. He tapped the side of his head.

"She's lost her memory," he whispered.

Lucky for me I hadn't lost my hearing.

"That knock on the head must have done it."

"Oh, no," said Mrs. Hershey. Her cheeks went pink. "What shall I do? The poor thing." She glanced at me.

"Try to make her comfortable until her memory returns," Dr. Oliver said.

He turned to me. "Mrs. Hershey loves children, Gracie," he said. "I'm sure you can see that."

I nodded.

"It seems you are going to be staying with her for a while. So you'd best treat her well," the doctor said.

"I will," I said.

Mrs. Hershey sat beside me and stroked my hair. "Of course you will."

Mrs. Hershey was sweet. Like chocolate.

And soft-spoken.

And nice.

"She's a little girl," Mrs. Hershey said. She smiled at the doctor. "What harm could she do?"

Then her smile dimmed.

"Is it all right that she talks to animals?"

Dr. Oliver packed up his leather bag.

"You mean her brother, the rat?" He chuckled. "That's her imagination working," he said. "Nothing to worry about, Kitty. Right Gracie?"

Whew!

"Right," I said.

"So let her get out of bed," Dr. Oliver said. "Let her help you around the house. It'll do you both good."

I threw back the covers.

Mrs. Hershey took my hand and helped me up. "I think what you need are some sweet caramels,

Gracie. Candy makes everything so much better."
She winked. "How does that sound?"

"Great," I said. I smoothed out the wrinkles in
my dress. Caramels would be tasty. And George
would be so mad when he found out.

"Lizzy," Mrs. Hershey called.

A short, plump woman wearing an apron walked
into the room. Her white hair was pulled back into a
bun. Her skirts swished as she walked.

"Can I get something for you, Mrs. Hershey?"
Lizzy said.

"Yes, thank you," said Mrs. Hershey. "Can you
bring the candy crock to the sitting room, please?"

"Happy to," said Lizzy. She left the room.

"We'll walk you out, Dr. Oliver," Mrs. Hershey
said.

I followed her and Dr. Oliver through the house
on our way to the front door.

It was huge, that place. Rooms everywhere.
Filled with beautiful furniture and paintings and
stuff. Like our museum back home.

Mrs. Hershey paused at a set of double doors.

"This is where my old rug was, Gracie," she said.

The Mom and Dad rug. I sucked in air with a big
glob of spit. I coughed.

Mrs. Hershey slapped me on the back.

"Dr. Oliver?" she said. "She's choking."

"Kitty," Dr Oliver said. "The child is fine. Please stop worrying."

"I'm . . . okay," I said. Then I looked in the room.

"Did Matthew and his white poodle come in here?" I said.

"Yes, they did," Mrs. Hershey said. She stopped talking, like she was remembering. "She was such a pretty dog." Mrs. Hershey smoothed my hair.

I touched my locket. Inside Mom had engraved the words, *To Gracie. Love, Mom.*

"And a smart dog, too," Mrs. Hershey said. "She seemed interested in that rug. Why, she rolled all over it. Then she barked at Matthew. Such a smart dog."

Dr. Oliver snorted. "We seem to be surrounded by smart animals. The next thing we know, the cows will be giving us chocolate milk."

Mrs. Hershey laughed. "That would solve Milton's problem," she said.

"Tell me more about Laura and Matthew," I said. "Please?"

Lizzy came back in carrying a gray jar with four blue stripes painted on it. She gave it to Mrs.

Hershey. "The candy crock, ma'am," she said.

"Thank you, Lizzy," Mrs. Hershey said.

"You're welcome," said Lizzy. And she swished out the double doors.

Mrs. Hershey pulled out three large caramels wrapped in paper from the jar.

"I know you're going to love these, Dr. Oliver," Mrs. Hershey said. "They're coated in chocolate."

Dr. Oliver stared at the caramels. "Your husband is a genius," he said.

She smiled and handed me and Dr. Oliver each a candy. Then she set the crock on a table.

"Milton made them this morning," she said. "From a new recipe. Top secret."

She winked.

Dr. Oliver raised his eyebrows and nodded.

Mrs. Hershey handed me a candy. Dr. Oliver slipped the chocolate caramel into his pocket.

"For later," he said, when he saw me watching.

"Did Matthew say anything else?" I said to Mrs. Hershey. Had Dad given Mrs. Hershey a message for me and George?

"Yes, he did, Gracie," she said. "He wished us well in the candy bar business.

"Dad always loved chocolate," I said. "Especially

Hershey bars. The giant size with almonds."

The kitchen went quiet.

"What did you say?" Mrs. Hershey said.

I clapped a hand over my mouth.

Dr. Oliver stared at me like I was a talking rat. Or something worse.

Oopsie. *Think, Gracie. Think.*

"Um, what?" I said.

"You said your dad loves Hershey bars," Mrs. Hershey said. "With almonds. But Mr. Hershey has never made such a candy."

"I said that? I don't remember," I said. Then I hit myself in the head. Three times.

Mrs. Hershey glanced at Dr. Oliver.

He tapped his forehead. "The accident," he said. "She might forget some things."

"Right," Mrs. Hershey said.

In slow motion I opened the caramel. I thought of Mom and Dad.

Did they wait for us somewhere close by? Were they even here?

Mrs. Hershey sat down on a velvet couch. "I'm feeling a bit weak," she said. "Will you see yourself out, Dr. Oliver?"

"Maybe I'll stay a bit longer," he said. He walked

over to Mrs. Hershey and took her wrist. He looked at his watch. "Hmm . . ." is all he said.

Mrs. Hershey patted the couch. "Sit here, Gracie," she said.

I sat next to her. I wanted to ask more about Mom and Dad. But I had to be careful about what I said now. No more mistakes.

I swallowed. "Mrs. Hershey. Are Matthew and his dog still around?"

"Oh, I doubt it, dear," she said. "They seemed to have important business back home."

Yes, they do have important business at home. It's called me and George and Grandpa.

I stared out the window. The sun was setting. Shadows from the trees moved in the wind.

Then a shadow creeped across the lawn.

I leaned forward in my chair.

The hair on the back of my neck stood up. I gripped the arms of the chair tight.

Crowe. Where was my rat brother when I needed him?

CHAPTER 7

Three Blind Mice . . . and One Rat

Mr. Hershey's laboratory was big and . . . messy. A lot messier than my bedroom.

The room was painted white. But it didn't have any windows. Not a single one. The wooden counters were piled high with dirty dishes. A whole bunch of empty glass milk bottles were stacked in a corner. Two giant brown bags leaned against one wall.

Mr. Hershey's laboratory reminded me of our kitchen back home.

After Mom and Dad disappeared, Grandpa and

me and Gracie tried to keep the house clean. But we aren't always good at it.

I missed home and Grandpa. I missed Mom and Dad.

And food.

Food would be good right now.

I sat up on my haunches.

I smelled cooked milk.

My stomach growled louder.

"For a small rat you do make a big noise," said Mr. Hershey.

He set me on a counter next to a copper bowl. It was big enough for two men to sit in. And it smelled like milk. In fact, almost everything in the laboratory smelled like milk and sugar and chocolate.

Mr. Hershey tied on an apron. He filled the copper bowl with milk. Then he lifted one of the bags and set it on the counter. Sugar fell out of it.

"You see this?" He put his hand on the bowl. A long wooden paddle leaned against one side.

I looked back at him. I wiggled my nose. And straightened my glasses. But I didn't answer.

"This is where I will make delicious chocolate candy that everyone in America can afford to buy. The good kind. Like they make in Switzerland and

France." He rubbed his eyes and forehead. "If I can get the recipe right."

Mr. Hershey struck a match and lit a fire under the giant bowl. "All right, George," he said. "We start by cooking the milk. Then we add the sugar."

He stirred the milk with the paddle.

"I bet I've cooked the milk and added the sugar a thousand times." He checked the flame. "But I still can't figure out how to make milk chocolate that melts in your mouth. And won't spoil on the market shelf. I've got to find the right formula."

I folded my paws under my chin and listened. The smell of warm milk made me sleepy.

"A lot of candy companies think I've discovered the recipe, " he said. The milk rippled as he stirred. "They're always sending people around. To spy on me."

Mr. Hershey shrugged. "That's why we keep so many secrets here."

I tried to cheer up Mr. Hershey. "*Eeep!*" I said.

It worked. He grinned. "Oh, forgive me, George. I'm going on and on when you're starving. I'll be right back with some bread and cheese for you."

He set the paddle down and left the room.

Now Mr. Hershey's laboratory was quiet. Except

for a clock ticking.

The flame crackling under the copper bowl.

And my stomach growling.

I felt a little nervous.

Crowe could be anywhere.

Maybe whistling would help.

So I whistled "Three Blind Mice."

Three blind mice, three blind mice.

Mr. Hershey sure was taking a long time getting that bread and cheese.

See how they run. See how they run.

A sound came from outside the door. Was it Crowe? He'd seen me driving the car with Gracie. He knows we're here.

And he knows I'm the rat.

I whistled faster.

They all ran after the farmer's wife.

Footsteps. I heard footsteps.

My whiskers twitched. My little rat heart went blip-blip-blip.

She cut off their tales with a . . .

My rat hairs stood straight up on my back.

. . . carving knife . . .

"A carving knife?" I said out loud. "That's it. I'm out of here."

I scurried behind the bag of sugar to hide.

Somebody jingled keys on the other side of the door.

I peeked out.

"Please don't be Crowe. With a carving knife," I whispered. I pulled my tail close around my body.

I squeezed my eyes almost shut.

The doorknob turned.

CHAPTER 8

Dark Shadows

The shadow stopped beneath the window. The one near me and Mrs. Hershey and Dr. Oliver.

Had he been listening to us?

"It's so nice to have you here, Gracie," Mrs. Hershey said. "You know, Mr. Hershey and I don't have any children."

I kept my eyes on the shadow. All the while my heart beat wild in my chest. I had a hard time listening to what Mrs. Hershey said.

She let out a sigh. "Milton has his business and we have each other. But no babies." She gave me a sad smile.

Dr. Oliver patted Mrs. Hershey's hand. "There, there, Kitty," he said. "You're tired, that's all."

Right then I felt sorry for Mrs. Hershey.

She closed her eyes. "I suppose you're right, Dr. Oliver. I may need to lie down for a while," she said.

"Let's leave Mrs. Hershey alone, Gracie," Dr. Oliver said.

"I hope you feel better," I said. "I should go find my broth—I mean, my rat, anyway."

Mrs. Hershey nodded. "Of course," she said. "Dr. Oliver? Do you mind taking her to Milton's laboratory?"

She handed him a ring of keys.

"I'd be happy to, Kitty," he said. "Please. Get some rest."

Dr. Oliver and I walked out the back door.

It was dark now. I couldn't see much.

But I knew someone was still out here. Somewhere in the shadows.

I followed Dr. Oliver across the dirt yard toward a big building. Two men stood at the doors.

"That's Milton's laboratory. And those men guard it," Dr. Oliver said. He bent down and whispered in my ear. "There are spies everywhere."

"Spies?" I said. I glanced from side to side. "You

mean like a tall guy? With dark hair? And gray eyes?"

"No. I mean *like you*, Miss Gracie." He squeezed my arm. "If that's who you really are."

"Me? I'm no spy," I said. "You mean Crowe." I tried to pull away.

"I'm not talking about birds here, Missy."

"Crowe's a man," I said.

"Well, I don't know any Crowe," Dr. Oliver said.

I pulled free.

"But I do know that you and your rat brother just happened to show up. All of a sudden." Dr. Oliver waved his hands around in the air. "In the middle of Milton's secret experiments."

"Don't try to deny it," he said. "You know more than you're letting on."

"No I don't," I said. I tapped my head like Dr. Oliver had tapped his. "I don't remember a thing. Remember?"

He narrowed his eyes. And tightened his lips.

We walked on.

I needed George now. The little rat.

At the door to the laboratory, Dr. Oliver took out the ring of keys.

"Dr. Oliver," said one of the guards. He nodded.

Dr. Oliver nodded back.

I couldn't see the other man. He kept his head low. And his hat covered his eyes. He didn't say a word.

He gave me the willies.

"I'll let you into the building, Gracie," Dr. Oliver said. "For Mrs. Hershey's sake. But remember, I'll be watching you. And your little rat, too."

I stared at the ground. Pretended like I didn't remember anything.

He unlocked one door and then another.

"Mind yourself now," he said. Then he left.

My knees shook.

I knocked on the closed door. "G-George?" I said. My voice shook, too. "Mr. Hershey?"

No answer.

The yummy smell of chocolate filled the air. That little rat. While Dr. Oliver was scaring me to pieces George was probably filling his pointy little face with chocolate.

If I wasn't so mad I might have been jealous.

I turned the knob and pushed open the door.

I heard a shrill scream.

And I saw George fall over in a dead rat faint. Again.

CHAPTER 9

Sugar and Spice and Not So Nice

Everything went black.

Then I heard Gracie's voice. "George. Wake up, George."

She poked me in the gut. "George? Are you dead or what?"

I opened my eyes and grabbed my tail. "Don't chop it off!" I said.

"What are you talking about?" said Gracie.

Her face was close to my nose. Her breath smelled like caramels.

"Somebody was trying to break into Mr. Hershey's laboratory. And he had a carving knife . . . I think."

"You were having a bad dream," said Gracie. "Who would want your nasty old tail?"

"Me, for starters," I said. "For now, anyway." I held onto my tail tight.

"Never mind about your dumb old rat dreams, George," Gracie said. She leaned down even closer to me. "I have something to tell you."

"Okay," I said. "What?" I straightened my glasses.

She looked from side to side.

So I looked from side to side.

Gracie fingered her locket. Her eyes almost popped out of her head.

I held my tail closer. "What's wrong with you?" I said.

"We're in some big trouble, George," she said.

"Tell me about it," I said. My stomach growled. It sounded like a garbage disposal now. "I'm starving."

"Who cares?" Gracie said. "I'm talking about Dr. Oliver. He thinks we're spies."

"Us? Spies?" I said. That didn't make any sense.

I scratched my hairy head with one claw.

"He's watching us, George," Gracie said. "What if he tells Mrs. Hershey and Mr. Hershey that we're spies? What if they believe him? What will happen to us?" She had her worried face on. "We have to get out of this place. We have to get the time machine and go home. Now."

She pulled hard on her locket chain. She was practically choking herself.

I slapped her hand with my claw. "Stop that," I said.

"That's not all, George," she said. "I have more bad news. I think I saw Crowe sneaking around the Hershey's house.

"Drat," I said.

"Double drat, you mean," said Gracie.

"Who does Dr. Oliver think we're spying on?" I said.

"He thinks we want Mr. Hershey's secret milk chocolate recipe," Gracie said.

"But he doesn't have one," I said, "yet."

"Let's go, George," Gracie said. "Before Dr. Oliver calls the police. We already gave the rug back, so we can leave now."

"As soon as the car is fixed," I said.

"Oh, no, George," said Gracie. She sounded like

she might cry. "I forgot about Lancaster. This is hopeless. We'll never see Mom and Dad or Grandpa again."

"Don't worry, Gracie," I said. "We'll find the time machine. Then maybe Mom and Dad will find us. Like last time."

Gracie's eyes got bright. "That's right, George," she said. "They did find us. What are you waiting for? Let's get going."

"Okay, okay," I said. My stomach made a whining sound. I still hadn't eaten. I looked at the bag of sugar on the counter. "In a second."

I scrambled up the bag to get a taste. It wobbled and tipped. I guess I was a fatter rat than I thought.

I slipped fast toward the copper bowl full of milk. "Whoa," I said.

"George, look out," Gracie said. She lunged forward and caught me . . . just in time.

The whole bag of sugar spilled into Mr. Hershey's milk.

"Uh-oh," we both said.

"Now you've done it, George," Gracie said in a whisper.

I felt sick. Mr. Hershey doesn't add the sugar until *after* the milk is cooked. He would never get his recipe right now.

Gracie held me up by the tail. "You and your stomach."

Then BOING. I had another brilliant idea. "Stir the sugar until it disappears, Gracie," I said. "Maybe the milk was already cooked all the way. Or close enough."

"Good idea, George," Gracie said. She set me back on the counter and picked up the wooden paddle. "Mr. Hershey will be glad we helped out."

Gracie stuffed the bag in a drawer. Then she stirred and stirred the milk.

"That was a *lot* of sugar," I said. My nose twitched with happiness. I couldn't help it. The smell of food made me happy.

Mr. Hershey walked in a while later.

Gracie hid the paddle behind her back.

I smiled and showed him all my teeth.

He smiled back.

"Hello, George," Mr. Hershey said. "And Gracie."

He carried a plate with cheese and apple slices on it.

I drooled. Just a little bit.

"How did you get in the laboratory?" he said.

"Did Kitty let you in?"

"No, sir," said Gracie. Her voice was small. She stood in front of the bowl, still holding the paddle behind her back.

No sir? I thought. When did *she* get so polite?

"Dr. Oliver let me in."

Mr. Hershey frowned. "Kitty gave Oliver the keys? I don't like that," he said. "I don't like that at all."

I looked at the apples and cheese. "*Eeep!*" I said.

"Oh, sorry, George," said Mr. Hershey. He set the plate down in front of me.

Gracie leaned the paddle against the counter.

I tried to stuff a whole piece of cheese into my mouth. It was too big, though. So I had to nibble. Fast.

"Isn't Dr. Oliver your friend, Mr. Hershey?" Gracie said.

"Oh yes. We have been friends for years," Mr. Hershey said. "I met him before I sold my caramel business. But that doesn't matter. I don't let *anyone* have those keys. "

"BURP!" I said. I finished the cheese and nibbled on an apple slice.

Mr. Hershey slipped into a white laboratory coat.

He stepped toward the big bowl. Then he frowned.

He rubbed his forehead. "Where's the bag of sugar I put on the counter?" he said.

Gracie shot me a look. A guilty one. And kept quiet.

I kept nibbling my apple and pretended to be a rat. A rat who did not spill sugar.

"I must be tired. I thought I had already put sugar right here." He touched the table and shook his head. Then he pulled another bag of sugar over to the bowl.

"How would you like to help me with a little experiment, Gracie?" Mr. Hershey said.

"Me?" Gracie said.

"Yes, you," said Mr. Hershey. "I think I can trust you."

"*Eeep!*" I said.

He didn't know that Dr. Oliver thought we were spies.

Or that my mother was a dog.

Or that we were all from the future.

"You, too, George," said Mr. Hershey. "Sometimes I hire children to help me with my work. Children are good secret keepers. Maybe rats are, too."

He winked at Gracie.

"What do you want me to do?" Gracie said.

Mr. Hershey turned up the flame under the bowl of milk. "Stir this milk until it gets nice and hot," he said. "Then we add the sugar. If all goes well, this batch will make the best milk chocolate in the world."

"Everybody loves your candy bars," Gracie said.

"*Eeep!*" I said. I shook my head at Gracie.

She looked nervous around the eyes. "I mean, *I bet* everyone will love them," she said.

"Thank you, Gracie," said Mr. Hershey. "Maybe you'll be my lucky charm. Maybe this time my recipe will work right."

"*Eeep!*" I said. My nose twitched and twitched at that one.

"Okay," she said. She swallowed hard and picked up the paddle. "I am a pretty good stirrer."

I jammed another apple slice in my mouth. I didn't want to all of a sudden *Eeep!* at Gracie again.

Gracie stirred and stirred. She had a guilty smile on her face the whole time.

I had a guilty stomach.

After a few minutes, Gracie stopped to rest.

"Are your arms tired?" Mr. Hershey asked.

Gracie nodded.

I nodded, too, because my arms were tired from lifting apple slices and cheese to my mouth.

"Let me try for a while," he said to Gracie.

He stirred and stirred.

I lay down on the counter and listened to my stomach go slosh, slosh, gurgle. "Ughh . . . "

"This milk seems so heavy," Mr. Hershey said. He tasted it. "And sweet." He frowned.

Gracie whistled.

I whistled, too.

Mr. Hershey folded his arms. "Okay, you two," he said. "Do you have something to tell me?"

I stood up. "It wasn't my fault," I said.

Mr. Hershey's eyes bugged out. His mouth dropped open.

But I ignored him. I paced back and forth on the counter. "I was so hungry and the sugar, was, well, there and everything. And anyway, Gracie stirred it in."

I only stopped talking to take a breath.

Maybe my last one.

Gracie glared at me. "Well, you blew it didn't you, George?" she said. "I hope you can get a ride home 'cause I'm not driving you."

"Me too," I said.

Mr. Hershey looked as if he'd heard a talking rat.

"George. You can talk," Mr. Hershey said.

"Oh, um. I guess so," I said. I grinned. My whiskers twitched. My little rat lips felt weak.

"We're sorry about the sugar, Mr. Hershey," said Gracie. "It was an accident. And yeah, George can talk. Unfortunately."

"That's all right, Gracie," he said. But he didn't take his eyes off me. "A talking rat," he said. He rubbed his temples. "We'd better keep this between us three," he said. "I don't think anyone else will understand. I don't think I understand."

"That's a great idea," Gracie said.

I squeezed my mouth shut and nodded. I was not a blabber rat.

"George agrees," said Gracie.

Mr. Hershey's milk bubbled in the pot. His face went funny. Like he had a BOING of an idea.

"The milk is heavy," he said. He tasted the milk again. "And sweet. Heavy and sweet."

Then he grinned. "The sugar goes in *before* you condense the milk. Before, before, before."

He danced around the room.

"Eureka," he yelled. "I've got it."

He hugged Gracie. Then he shook my paw. "You two *are* my lucky charms. I've done it. I mean, we've done it. We've found the recipe for milk chocolate at last."

I couldn't help it. I was so happy for Mr. Hershey that I sang out loud. And dancing a little ratty jig.

"We've done it. We've done it. We've done it!"

The door opened.

And in walked Sid.

"Mr. Hershey," he said.

I scrambled up Gracie's arm.

Sid scowled at us. "Mrs. Hershey sent me to get Gracie and George," he said. "She says it's long past time for their dinner."

Gracie shivered.

So did I.

Then BOING! I had another one of my ideas.

Of all the people on the Hershey farm, Sid seemed most like a spy to me.

A big, mean spy. A spy who didn't like me or Gracie.

Here were the facts: He was always hanging around watching people. And following people. He was never far away from Mr. Hershey or the laboratory.

And now me and Gracie knew Mr. Hershey's secret recipe.

The recipe a spy like Sid would do anything to get.

"Oh, very well," said Mr. Hershey. "I suppose I have a long night ahead of me anyway. Plenty of work to do."

He stepped over to me and Gracie and leaned down. "I'll bring you two the first chocolate bar made from our brand new recipe," he said.

He winked.

Then Sid pushed us out the door.

CHAPTER 10

George is Really a Chicken

Sid and I walked down the dark hall outside Mr. Hershey's laboratory. George rode on my shoulder.

"He's the spy," George said in my ear.

I stopped walking.

George nearly fell.

"Get a move on," Sid said.

I stared right at him.

His eyebrows were too bushy.

His face was too frown-y.

He didn't seem nice at all.

George was right. All the time Mr. Hershey worried about spies. And a spy *worked* for him.

George's whiskers tickled my neck.

Why couldn't George have turned into a mountain lion or a polar bear? No, he had to be an eensy weensy rat. And I was leaving with a mean looking guy.

"If he tries to grab you," George said. "Run." His breath smelled like apples. "Run as fast as you can."

"Thanks a lot, George," I said. "You're a big help. Okay, a *little* help."

"I may be little. But I have sharp teeth." George clacked his teeth together.

"That's great, George. Maybe you can nibble him to death," I whispered.

My knees shook. How fast could I run in this dress?

"What did you say?" Sid said.

He stared at me. Then at George. Then at me again.

"Nothing," I said.

George clacked his teeth at Sid.

Our footsteps echoed in the hall.

We were to the last door now. The one that would lead outside to freedom.

Sid bent down. Way down. Till he was looking me straight in the eye.

"Missy," he said. His breath did *not* smell like apples. "Missy, you had better not cause any mischief for Mr. Hershey."

I felt George tremble. He moved from my one shoulder to the other. My brother the rat was really a chicken.

"Get ready to run," George said in my other ear.

I was ready to run all right. I took a step toward the door. Then I stopped.

And turned back to Sid.

"What are you doing?" George said. "Run!"

But I didn't.

I made my back as straight as I could.

"I like Mrs. Hershey," I said to Sid. "I like her a lot. And Mr. Hershey, too. I don't want their chocolate recipe. The rat and me, we're looking for our parents."

George dug his claws into my shoulder.

"Ouch."

Sid's bushy eyebrows climbed up his forehead like they were caterpillars. Live ones.

"We're not chocolate thieves, Sid," I said.

Then I opened the door myself.

We stepped into the dark night.

Sid didn't say a word.

Without looking back, I walked me and George toward the house. And Mrs. Hershey.

The air outside was warm and smelled like clover. A breeze blew. The sun had settled down and now the moon was up. It looked like the color of the milk Mr. Hershey had cooked in the laboratory.

In front of us was the Hershey house. I could see the lights on in the kitchen.

"Wow, Gracie," George said, from his chicken roost on my shoulder. "That was pretty cool. You stood right up to that bully Sid."

For some reason, I felt like crying. I wanted Mom and Dad. I wanted Grandpa. I wanted to be home. But I already missed Mrs. Hershey.

"Let's find the time machine," I said. "Mom and Dad won't be far away from wherever it is."

Then I heard a chewing noise. I stopped.

"George, what are you eating now?" I said.

"Nothing."

I felt a tug. "George?" I said.

"Okay, okay. It's your hair," he said. "But I'm not eating it. I'm flossing."

"Aargh! Stop it," I said.

Sid called out to us. "Hey there."

I turned around real slow. What did he want now?

"Sid's a big guy," George said. "He might run faster than that car we drove this morning."

"Be quiet, George," I said.

Sid still stood in the doorway of Mr. Hershey's laboratory.

He almost filled the opening, he was so big. I couldn't see his face in the dark.

He looked like a huge, scary shadow.

"I believe you," he said.

Then he walked back into the building, closing the door behind him.

"What's that?" George said.

"That," I said, "was Sid. Being . . . nice." I couldn't believe it.

"No," George said. "That sound. What was that sound?"

"Are you still chewing on my hair?" I said. "Because if I wind up bald . . . "

"It sounds like someone's sneaking up on us," he said.

He put his paws on my neck.

"Quit trying to scare me, George," I said. Shivers

ran over my arms. I took bigger steps. "We're almost to the house. Then we'll be safe."

I saw Mrs. Hershey pull the kitchen curtains closed. Now all I had to see by was the milky moon.

"Here we are," a voice said. It came from the darkness. "All alone at last."

I gave a jump of surprise.

"*Eeep!*" George said.

He slid down my shoulder.

"I told you I heard something," he said.

"So you're not alone. You have the rat. How amusing," the voice said.

Crowe stepped out of the shadows.

His gray eyes kind of glowed in the light of the moon.

He was the other man guarding Mr. Hershey's laboratory with Sid. A shiver ran from my head to my toes.

"I felt that," said George.

Dr. Oliver moved from behind Crowe.

Before I had a chance to move, Crowe grabbed me by the arm.

"Come with me, Gracie, my dear," he said between clenched teeth. "We have a little meeting with Time."

I dug my boot heels into the ground. "I'm not going anywhere with you," I said.

Dr. Oliver came up on the other side.

"Yes, you will," Dr. Oliver said.

"You're working *together*?" George said.

"In a way, my little rat friend," Crowe said.

"I'm pretending I didn't hear that rat talk," Dr. Oliver said.

The two men pulled George and me to the barn.

"I'm helping Dr. Oliver here with a special cooking secret," said Crowe. "And he's helping me find a special machine."

My heart thumped.

We were almost to the barn now. It was dark as a cave. And still smelly.

"Let go of me," I said. I tried to shake free.

"According to the workers here on Hershey's farm," Dr. Oliver said, "the girl and the rat arrived in the automobile."

"I *know* that, Oliver," said Crowe. His voice was impatient. "I saw them with my own eyes. I want to know where the blasted thing is now."

We all stood in the pale moonlight.

"In the barn," said Dr. Oliver. "The men decided to take it to Lancaster in the morning." He wiped his forehead with his handkerchief. "It's still broken," he said.

Crowe spoke in a soft voice. "Let's all find out if the time machine works, shall we?" He squeezed my arm. His face was hard. His mouth a thin line.

George ran down my arm. He clawed Crowe's hand.

"She's not going anywhere with you," George said.

Crowe gave George a smile. "But you're coming, too. I would hate to separate you from your sister."

Dr. Oliver's eyes went wide. "So that rat really *is* her brother? And he can talk?" he said.

"That's not all I can do," George said. "So you'd better not get too close. Or else." He showed all his teeth to Dr. Oliver.

Dr. Oliver shook his head. "I'll forget the rat in the morning."

"Mrs. Hershey is expecting us," I said. "She'll send someone to find us."

Dr. Oliver picked George up by his tail. "Then we'd better hurry, hadn't we?" he said.

CHAPTER 11

Rat Fink

"I'm going to throw up," I said.

The apples and cheese in my stomach sloshed around. My head felt like a brick from hanging upside down.

"Stop that! You're hurting George," Gracie said. She tried to yank herself away from Crowe. But she couldn't get free.

"George will be fine," Crowe said. "As long as you do what I tell you to do."

"I'll scream," Gracie said. She opened her mouth wide.

"Go ahead," said Dr. Oliver. "But if you do," he

held me up high in the air, "the rat gets it."

"*Eeep!*" I said.

I scratched the air with my claws. But I couldn't grab anything to hold on to.

This was it. I was going to die. The End.

"No, don't," said Gracie. "You let him go!"

"Give me the recipe first," Dr. Oliver said.

"Give her the rat, Oliver," said Crowe. "There's no need to scare the children. They'll do what they're told. Won't you?"

His voice was softer. He sounded almost nice. He let go of Gracie's arm.

My whiskers didn't trust him. And neither did I.

"I had a feeling you two were trouble the first time I saw you," Dr. Oliver said. He handed me over to Gracie.

She put me in her dress pocket.

"Let's get this over with," said Dr. Oliver. "I want Hershey's milk chocolate recipe, quick. The sooner you're out of my hair, the better." He looked over his shoulder.

"He doesn't have any hair," I said.

Gracie patted my head. Her hand was all sweaty.

I held her finger with both my paws. "Don't be afraid, Gracie," I said. "I'm here with you."

"You can't have Mr. Hershey's recipe," said Gracie. "It's not yours."

"Yeah," I said.

"I've got news for you two." Dr. Oliver lowered his voice. "The chocolate recipe is as much mine as it is Hershey's. I've been with him longer than anyone, even Kitty. Since the caramel business."

"And what about Mr. Hershey and Mrs. Hershey?" Gracie said, "They're your friends."

Gracie didn't sound so scared anymore. She sounded mad.

Dr. Oliver laughed.

"Maybe I like money more than friends," he said. "And this recipe will make me rich."

"Mr. Hershey was right not to trust you," Gracie said.

"You told me you could deal with these children," Dr. Oliver said to Crowe.

Crowe just smiled. His arms were crossed.

Dr. Oliver gritted his teeth. In a low voice, he said, "You and your little rat brother can make this easy on yourselves," he said. He came closer. He pointed a fat finger in Gracie's face. "Or you can make it hard. Tell me what you know about Hershey's secret recipe. This instant."

Gracie pulled on her locket. But she didn't say a word.

Dr. Oliver gave her a shake. "Tell me what you know."

"Let go of me," Gracie said.

"Oh no you don't," he said. "I've waited a long time for this."

"Let go of her, Oliver," said Crowe. His voice boomed in the barn. "I need them both unharmed."

Dr. Oliver jumped. He dropped his hold on Gracie. He took a step back.

He was scared of Crowe, too.

"Now Gracie," Crowe said. His voice sounded like warm milk and sugar. "Give Dr. Oliver what he wants. We'll find your parents. Then we can all go home. Together."

Gracie's eyes brightened. "You know where Mom and Dad are?"

What was she doing? "It's a trick, Gracie," I said. "Don't believe him."

My heart beat like popping corn. What if I was wrong? What if Crowe *did* know about Mom and Dad? He might be the only one who could help us.

My whiskers twitched. A lot. I trusted my whiskers.

"Shh," said Gracie. She pushed me down into her pocket.

I nibbled on her finger. "Ouch, stop it, George," she said.

"You're not listening, Gracie," I said.

"Can't you make the rat stop talking?" said Dr. Oliver. He sat on a bale of hay and put his head in his hands.

"I don't blame you for not trusting me, George,"

Crowe said. "But I can prove it. As soon as the two of you climb into the time machine, your parents will appear. Isn't that what happened last time?"

Crowe was right about that, at least.

Gracie narrowed her eyes. I could tell she was thinking things over, too.

My rat sense was telling me, *Don't do it, George. Don't get in that car with Crowe.*

But Gracie couldn't hear my rat sense. She couldn't feel my heart bee-bopping. She didn't notice my whiskers moving like egg beaters.

Nope. She wasn't paying attention to any of that.

She was too busy . . . walking us both to the time machine.

CHAPTER 12

Left Behind

George scrambled out of my pocket and up my arm.

"Don't do this, Gracie," he said. "Something is not right."

My guts told me the same thing. But I ignored them. And George.

I wanted to see Mom and Dad.

I wanted to go home. For good.

A tiny bit of moonlight spilled in through the open barn doors. But it was still so dark inside. I couldn't see the car.

I mean, the time machine.

Crowe struck a match. His face looked orange in

the light of the flame. "Ah, there it is in the corner," he said. He motioned with his hand. "After you, children."

I walked with him to the time machine.

Then I stopped. "You have to promise to help us bring Mom and Dad home," I said. "Or else I'm not going anywhere."

"Of course," said Crowe. "That's all part of my plan. I can't help them if they're not here, can I? So climb in and they'll come."

"Nobody's going anywhere until I get that recipe," said Dr. Oliver. He stepped up beside Crowe. "We had a deal."

"You'll get your recipe, Oliver," said Crowe. "Be patient." He reached out to me. "Let me help you in, Gracie."

I wanted to believe in Crowe. I gave him my hand.

A rat voice shouted in my ear. "Stop, Gracie! Don't get in the car."

I stopped. Was George right? Or Crowe?

"Our Grandpa doesn't trust you," George said to Crowe. "And neither do we."

"And for that matter, neither do I," said Dr. Oliver.

He slapped his hand down on Crowe's shoulder. Crowe ignored him.

"You'll be much safer inside, children," said Crowe. He opened the car door. "I'll deal with Dr. Oliver."

"See, George," I said. "Crowe's not the bad guy. Dr. Oliver is."

George stuck his nose right into my ear.

"Get ready," he said.

"Ready for what?" I said.

Crowe shook off Dr. Oliver's hand and leaped forward. He pushed me into the car with him. I fell on the floor, banging my shins.

The time machine made a whirring sound. Like a helicopter.

"It works!" Crowe said. "It works!" His voice made the hair on the back of my neck stand up. "I only needed you two children. After all these years, I can go home."

George was right about Crowe.

"Oh, no you don't," said Dr. Oliver. He tried to pull Crowe out of the car. Crowe knocked him back.

Everything happened fast after that.

I climbed up on the seat in the time machine where Crowe sat.

George jumped off my shoulder and landed on Crowe's head.

He clung to Crowe's hair. Biting and scratching.

"George," I said. "We're taking off."

The time machine shook. Lights flickered on and I saw the whole inside of the barn. Dr Oliver looked startled.

So did the cows.

"Jump out, Gracie," George said. "Hurry."

Crowe kicked at the doctor. George kept biting Crowe.

Dr. Oliver tried to pull Crowe out of the car. George was still on Crowe's head. "We made a deal," Dr. Oliver said. "I got you the children. Now give me the recipe." His voice was loud and screechy.

Like a big rat. A big rat fink.

Before I could get out of the car, a seat belt sprang out of the sides. It snapped over my lap.

"George," I said. "Jump!" But I could hardly hear my own voice. The time machine made a lot of noise.

Crowe swung at Dr. Oliver.

George covered Crowe's eyes with his furry body. His tail wrapped around Crowe's neck.

"You blasted rat." Crowe hollered so loud the

cows mooed.

Then the time machine tipped over.

And dumped Crowe out. George fell out with him.

I made a grab for George. But I missed. He landed on the ground next to Dr. Oliver.

The doors on the time machine slammed shut.

Crowe pulled at the handle. "You are not leaving me behind. Help me, Oliver."

But Dr. Oliver was chasing George. He tried to stomp on him. "Give me that recipe, Gracie. Or the rat gets it."

"Gets what?" said George.

"This," said Dr. Oliver and stepped on George's tail.

"*Eeep!*" said George.

"Zig zag, George," I said.

George zigged. Dr. Oliver zagged.

I tried to unsnap the seat belt, but the time machine wouldn't let me. "Let me go," I said.

"Stay there, Gracie," George said. "I'm coming."

He zigged again. Right up Dr. Oliver's pant leg.

"*Eeep!*" said Dr. Oliver. Then he zigged and zagged all over the barn.

The time machine shook so hard my teeth

rattled. Crowe held on tight.

Then, just like that, a white poodle with pink bows on her ears raced up and down in front of me.

"Mom," I said.

"Gracie," Mom said. Her voice was all poodle-y and . . . and wonderful.

And there was Dad. He looked so real. And tall. And handsome like always.

Dad ran toward Crowe and tackled him.

I tried harder to get out of the time machine.

Mom barked and ran around on her back legs.

Mr. Hershey and Sid ran into the barn. Mrs. Hershey followed them in her long dress.

"What's all the commotion?" Mr. Hershey said.

Sid jumped on Crowe. Mr. Hershey wrestled Dr. Oliver.

"Mom." I yelled now. I could feel tears on my cheeks. "Dad. George."

No one seemed to hear me.

The time machine began a slow spin around the barn. The lights came on.

Crowe and Sid were on the ground.

Mrs. Hershey stared at me. Her mouth was open in surprise. I pressed my hands to the window.

Dr. Oliver shook his leg. And George rolled out

onto the floor.

Mrs. Hershey scooped George up and held him like a baby. She petted him.

"Get in, George," I said. "Hurry."

"*Eeep!*" said George. He looked green.

Mom kept barking.

Mrs. Hershey blew a kiss at me.

Then ZOOM!

I was in a black hole.

All by myself.

CHAPTER 13

Home Alone

The time machine crashed to a stop.

The lights went dark.

It sputtered and made a g-a-s-p.

And coughed me out onto the floor.

I rolled to a stop at Grandpa's feet.

"Gracie," Grandpa said. He picked me up. "You're all right."

He squeezed me so tight I couldn't breathe.

"Yeah . . . Grandpa. I'm . . . okay," I said, crying.

I felt sick.

"Where's George?" Grandpa said.

I shook my head. "I don't know," I said.

Grandpa's face dropped. "Tell me what happened, Gracie," he said. "Tell me!"

"He didn't get in the car," I said. "I screamed for him. But he didn't get in."

The tears ran down my cheeks. "He didn't get in, Grandpa," I said again.

Grandpa put his arm around me. "Why not?" he said.

"He was trying to protect me," I said. "From Crowe."

Grandpa covered his face with his hands.

"I knew this would happen," he said.

I cried into Grandpa's work shirt. "I have to bring him back."

How could I get back to Hershey, Pennsylvania? We had returned the rug. Would the time machine know where to go?

"You're not going anywhere, Gracie," said Grandpa. "No one is getting in that machine ever again.

The time machine burped.

Me and Grandpa jerked around when we heard it.

"George?" we said at the same time.

The time machine was a cabinet with two giant doors on the front.

Me and Grandpa took a step toward it. Slow and careful.

Like we were sneaking up on a crocodile.

From behind.

I didn't trust crocodiles. And I didn't trust that time machine, either.

Then I remembered. It had tried to help us get rid of Crowe back there in the barn. Maybe it would help us again.

I took another step forward.

Grandpa put his hands on my shoulders. "Don't get in that thing," he said.

"Don't worry," I said.

I moved closer. The time machine purred.

"That's right," I said in a soft voice. "You know me, don't you?"

I took a deep breath. "We need you to go back for George." I talked loud. Like you do when you're talking to an old person who can't hear.

Grandpa turned to me. "Gracie," he said. "I'm not deaf."

"Not you, Grandpa," I said. "The time machine."

I took another step. I put my hand on the

doorknob. The machine lit up.

"I need you to take me to George," I said.

"No, Gracie," Grandpa said.

I leaped in the cabinet and slammed the doors shut.

"I'll be right back," I said. "With George."

"Gracie!" Grandpa said.

The machine shook.

My heart pounded. I had to get George, no matter how scared I was.

Grandpa banged on the outside of the cabinet. "Gracie!" He pulled hard on the doors.

Then I heard a loud sound. Like a lion roaring.

And ZOOM! I was back in a black hole.

CHAPTER THE END

A Strange New Friend

Here's the thing. I don't know what really happened.

Not everything, anyway.

I mean, first I was beating Crowe up.

I almost got stomped on. Plus I saw a super hairy leg.

Gracie and the time machine left without me. So for a minute I was stuck in time, too.

Then I saw my dad.

And my mom the poodle.

I tried to get to them. But Mrs. Hershey picked me up.

Dad waved and Mom said, "We miss you,

Georgie." In a twinkle, they were gone.

Mrs. Hershey said, "George. You've got to go home."

Then BAM! The time machine came back with Gracie. "Come on, George," she said. "Jump."

Mrs. Hershey tossed me to Gracie. "Goodbye, children," she said.

ZOOM! We got sucked into a dark place. I was upside down.

Then SWOOSH! Giant doors flew open. I rolled out onto the floor.

Followed by Gracie. She wore her blue jeans now.

She looked happy to see me. "George!" she said. She pushed me hard and laughed.

Grandpa pulled me up and gave me a big kiss on the forehead.

"Don't ever scare me like that again," Grandpa said.

"I'm sorry, Grandpa," she said. "But I had to go. I mean, we had to."

Grandpa ruffled my hair.

I am not a big fan of the hair ruffle.

But wait. Hair?

I had my hair back.

And *feet*! I was a real live boy again.

"Cool," I said.

"Why can't the time machine bring Mom and Dad back?" Gracie said. "I mean, by itself?"

Grandpa shook his head. "It's not that easy, honey."

Gracie pulled on her necklace. "Maybe if we say pretty please? With sugar on top?" she said.

Gracie was right. No more Crowe. No more dangerous missions. We could be a family again. Right now.

But Grandpa was more right.

"Gracie, you know we can't do that," I said. "We have to play by the rules. Mom and Dad can't come home. Not until you and me take back all the stuff they bought for the museum."

I looked back at the time machine. A big, stupid cabinet. It couldn't help us. No one could.

So me and Gracie would have to do this all by ourselves.

I closed my eyes. *We'll be back, Mom and Dad . . .*

The machine said, "Brrr-oop."

"Did you hear that, George?" Gracie said.

Grandpa smiled.

Gracie bit her lip. "So, where do we go next, Grandpa?"

taptap tap-tap taptap tap-tap

The three of us looked at the telegraph machine.

taptap tap-tap taptap tap-tap

"It's Mom and Dad," Gracie said. Her voice was a whisper.

"Here we go again," I said.

We all ran to the telegraph.

Grandpa grabbed a pad and pencil. He spoke as he wrote.

"George . . . and Gracie . . . home?"

Grandpa tapped out an answer. "Yes. . . . Kids . . . fine."

The telegraph went quiet.

"Come on," said Grandpa. He clenched his teeth. "Say something else."

But the telegraph stayed silent.

Grandpa shook his head. He was as quiet as the telegraph machine.

"We can do it, Grandpa," I said. "Like the Three Musketeers. One for all . . . "

I waited for Grandpa to finish the line.

"One for all . . . " Gracie said again. She waited, too.

Grandpa turned toward the map of the United States.

The little red light on the map lit up.

"Look," I said.

"Mom and Dad are trying to tell us where they are," Gracie said.

The light blinked.

And blinked.

And blinked some more.

Grandpa turned to me and Gracie.

" . . . and all for one," he said.

Then the three of us walked to the map.

THE END . . . OR IS IT?

Milton Hershey and His Chocolate Factory

"Hi. This is Gracie."

"And this is George. We're going to tell you the true story of Milton Hershey's Chocolate Factory. And I'm going to start. Right Gracie?"

"Right, George."

"Okay. Here goes. Milton Hershey was born on a farm in Derry Township, Pennsylvania in 1857. His father had a lot of different jobs, like farmer and cough-drop maker. Milton's dad moved the family around a lot, so Milton didn't get to go to school all the time. And he finally had to quit after the fourth grade."

"That's kind of sad, George."

"I know, Gracie. But don't worry. This story has a happy ending. Anyway, when Milton was only fourteen, his mom got him a job with a candy maker in Lancaster, Pennsylvania."

"Um, George. His mom got him an apprenticeship, not a job. He was like a student of the candy maker. And that's how he got interested in the candy business."

"Yeah, I was getting to that, Gracie, okay?"

"I was just saying."

"Now you did it, Gracie. I forgot what I was going to say."

"Big hint: Milton's caramel business."

"Oh, yeah. I remember now. When Milton turned nineteen years old, he borrowed money from his mom and his uncle to start a taffy and caramel business. But it didn't work out. Then he started another candy business. But he had to close that one, too. He tried one more time."

"And that one didn't work, either. Is it my turn yet, George?"

"Sheesh. Would you wait a second, Gracie? I'm almost done. Okay, finally Milton asked his friend for help, and they made the Lancaster Caramel Company. This time it worked out great. Milton decided to use the money he earned to start a chocolate business. Back then, chocolate candy cost a lot of money and only rich people could buy it. Milton wanted to make chocolate candy bars so cheap that everyone could afford one. He also wanted to make chocolate bars that wouldn't spoil sitting on the store shelves for a long time. Okay, Gracie. It's your turn. But don't take too long."

"Real nice, George."

"Thanks, Gracie."

"This is my favorite part, anyway. Milton tried hard for many years to find the right milk chocolate recipe for his candy."

"And he wasn't even a scientist, remember Gracie? He only finished fourth grade."

"That's right, George. Here's a candy bar to put in your mouth so I can talk."

"A Hershey bar. Thanks Gracie."

"But Milton was smart. He even built a candy factory and a secret laboratory so he could work on his recipes. He put guards around his laboratory while he worked. There were spies hanging around, you know, George."

"Gwmff, gwmff."

"Don't talk with your mouth full, George. It's not pretty. One fall night in 1903, Milton and his friend, John Schmalbach, discovered that they had to mix milk and sugar together at just the right time to get the best milk chocolate bars ever. And that's how Hershey's chocolate candy was invented. Ta-da."

"GULP. That's good chocolate. Can I have another one?"

"Maybe later, George. I have to tell them about Kitty. Then you have to tell them about Milton's town."

"All right. But hurry up. I'm starving."

"Wipe the chocolate off your glasses, George."

"Oh. No wonder you look all smudgy."

"Brother. Milton met Kitty—her real name was Catherine Sweeny—in New Jersey in 1898. She was twenty-six years old and so pretty and fun. They fell in love. And probably kissed."

"Yuck. I hate mushy stuff."

"Then they got married. Milton brought Kitty flowers every day. He probably kissed her every day, too."

"Ugh. I'm going to throw up, Gracie. No lie."

"Grow up, George. Kitty got sick and she couldn't

have children. So Milton and Kitty built a home for orphaned boys right in Hershey, Pennsylvania."

"Wow. That's nice."

"But here's the sad part, George. Kitty never got well and she died in 1915, way before Milton."

"Oh. Boy, Gracie. That is sad."

"Yeah."

"Should I tell them about the town now, Gracie?"

"I think so, George. Can you pass the tissues first?"

"Here you go. This is the last part of the story, and I'll hurry before Gracie starts bawling. Milton built this great town for the workers in his chocolate factory. Hey, Gracie. This'll make you laugh: Milton Hershey and the Chocolate Factory."

"Finish the story, okay George?"

"Party pooper. So Milton built nice houses and roads and schools and stores for his workers so they would be happy. He named the town Hershey, Pennsylvania. Milton Hershey was a nice person, Gracie."

"Yeah, he was, George. He even built a fun park in Hershey for his workers and their families. And now Hershey Park—that's the name of the fun park—is kind of like Disneyland and anybody can go there."

"Cool. Gracie?"

"What, George?"

"Can I have another Hershey bar now?"

"Say goodbye, George."

"Goodbye, George."

"Brother."

Pennsylvania State Facts

- **Statehood:** December 12, 1787, second state to ratify the Constitution.
- **Origin of the Name Pennsylvania:** Named to honor William Penn, Pennsylvania's founder.
- **State Capital:** Harrisburg
- **State Flag:** Deep blue background. In the center are two harnessed draft horses surrounding a shield picturing a ship, a plow, and three sheaves of wheat. Above is a bald eagle. Below are a stalk of corn, an olive branch, and a draped red ribbon that reads, "VIRTUE, LIBERTY, AND INDEPENDENCE."
- **State Nicknames:** "Keystone State," "Quaker State"
- **State Song:** "Pennsylvania," lyrics by Eddie Khoury, music by Ronnie Bonner
- **State Motto:** "Virtue, Liberty, and Independence"
- **State Flower:** Mountain laurel
- **State Tree:** Eastern hemlock
- **State Bird:** Ruffed grouse

- **State Animal:** White-tailed deer
- **State Insects:** Ladybug and firefly
- **State Colors:** Blue and gold

Pennsylvania State Curiosities

- Betsy Ross made the first American flag in Philadelphia, Pennsylvania in 1776.

- The Declaration of Independence was signed in Philadelphia, Pennsylvania in 1776.

- The Liberty Bell was made in England in 1753 and is located in Philadelphia, Pennsylvania. The bell was likely rung at the first public reading of the Declaration of Independence in Philadelphia (on July 8, 1776).

- Philadelphia, Pennsylvania was the United States capital city from 1790 to 1800.

- The Battle of Gettysburg, an important battle in the Civil War and the inspiration for President Lincoln's Gettysburg Address, took place near Gettysburg, Pennsylvania from July 1 to July 3, 1863.

- The Philadelphia Zoo was the first public zoo in the United States and opened on July 1, 1874.

- The first baseball stadium in America was built in

Pittsburgh, Pennsylvania in 1909.

- The Little League World Series started in South Williamsport, Pennsylvania in 1947. The Series is still played in St. Anne, Pennsylvania every August.

- *Mr. Roger's Neighborhood*, a popular children's television program, first aired on United States television on February 19, 1968 in Pittsburg, Pennsylvania. Mr. Rogers was born on March 20, 1928 in Latrob, Pennsylvania.

- Each year on Groundhog Day (February 2) in Punxsutawney, Pennsylvania, people from all over the U.S. watch Phil the Groundhog as he emerges from his burrow. If he sees his shadow that means we'll have six more weeks of winter.

Get a sneak peak of what happens next!

CHAPTER 1

Off to See the Wizard

I reached toward the blinking red light on Grandpa's map of the United States.

Here's the thing.

That map is pinned to Grandpa's fix-it-shop wall.

It's not plugged in anywhere.

So how's that light blinking?

How does it know where Mom and Dad are

now?

That's what I wanted to find out.

"Don't mess with that, George," Grandpa said. He reached for my shoulder. "You might get a shock. Or worse."

I had to know. I squinted and touched the map with my finger.

Nothing happened.

"Whew," I said. "Nope. No shock. It's not even hot." I tried to sound like No Big Deal. But my legs wobbled. A lot.

"Who cares about that?" Gracie said. "Stop goofing around, George. Read where we're going next. "

"Hold your horses . . . I mean, hold your *horse*, Gracie," I said. Then I laughed at my own joke. Because it was hilarious.

Grandpa covered a smile with his hand. "That never gets old," he said.

Gracie showed me her teeth. Like she did when she was a horse in Delaware. During the Revolutionary War. I backed up a step.

"Whatever, George," she said. But she smiled too.

Grandpa stood next to me and read the map. "Your mom and dad are in Menlo Park, New Jersey.

In 1879," he said.

The time machine shook and shivered. "Bl-l-rrrr," it said.

I jumped a mile.

So did Gracie. Right into me.

My glasses went all skewampus.

Grandpa didn't flinch. "Well I'll be," he said. He moved closer to the time machine.

The time machine looks like a regular old wardrobe now. But me and Gracie and Grandpa know better. In Delaware it looked like an outhouse. In Pennsylvania, it was a car. It is a master of disguise.

Grandpa smoothed its doors with his hand. "Menlo Park, New Jersey," he said again. The time machine shook harder than before. "Bl-l-rrrr," it said again.

That freaked me out because who knew it could talk?

"Grandpa, don't," said Gracie. She held tight to her locket. The one Mom gave her.

The time machine is scared of Menlo Park, New Jersey. Which is right where me and Gracie were going next. To save our parents.

Grandpa acted like he didn't hear Gracie. He walked to his desk and pulled out his big stack of papers. He wrote down everything Mom and Dad traveled back in time to buy for our family's museum. The Stockton Museum of Just About Everything in American History.

"I remember that place," Grandpa said. He ran his finger down a page. "Yes, here it is. *Little Women* by Louisa May Alcott. Published in 1868."

"Huh?" me and Gracie said at the same time.

"Jinx," Gracie said. "Ha! You owe me a soda."

"Ding dang it," I said.

"*Little Women*," Grandpa said. "It's a book. In our Books from America exhibit."

He walked out of the fix-it shop. Me and Gracie followed him into the dark museum. Past a Kermit the Frog puppet in the Sesame Street exhibit. Around the statue of John Wayne sitting on a horse. Past the electric guitar exhibit. The exit signs glowed green above the doorways.

Grandpa walked fast. So did Gracie. I hurried to catch up. We stopped at the Books from America exhibit. And I bumped right into Gracie.

"Ow!" we both said.

Gracie rubbed the back of her head.

I rubbed the front of my head.

"Jinx," I said. "Ha! You owe me a soda, Gracie."

"No. I don't," she said.

"Oh," I said. Because her voice sounded like a boxing glove. One that wanted to punch me in the nose.

Grandpa switched on a light. Bookshelves and books covered this corner of the museum. From the floor to the ceiling. Grandpa ran his finger along a wall of books. He pulled a brown one out of a shelf. "I traveled back in time with your parents when they bought this," he said. "In Menlo Park, New Jersey." He blew dust off the cover. "I met Thomas Edison there."

I stared at Grandpa. So did Gracie.

"The guy who invented electricity?" Gracie asked.

"Uh, Gracie," I said. I swallowed a super gigantic laugh. "Thomas Edison didn't invent electricity. He invented the light bulb." I tapped the side of my head. "Brains of the family, remember?"

Gracie frowned. "Whatever, George. Is he important?"

"Mr. Edison was a genius," said Grandpa. "The newspaper reporters at the time called him The Wizard of Menlo Park."

"Pretty important, I guess," said Gracie.

I gave her my twisted smile nod.

Grandpa opened the book. "See this?" he said and held it out to us.

Me and Gracie moved close to Grandpa.

I peered at the name "Thomas A. Edison" written in cursive on the first page. "Cool," I said.

"Wow," Gracie said. "How did you get that?" She traced the signature with her finger.

"I ran into Mr. Edison in a store in Menlo Park," said Grandpa. "Your mom and dad wanted to buy a book for the museum. That's when Mr. Edison walked in." Grandpa smiled. "I asked him to sign our book. He and I had a nice talk."

Grandpa is sort of a scientist. He can figure out how to fix anything in the museum. Maybe that's why he likes Thomas Edison so much.

When we got back to the fix-it shop, the time machine was quiet. I watched it as we walked past. But it didn't move. It didn't make a Bl-l-rrr.

It was after midnight. Way past bedtime. But me and Gracie couldn't go to bed yet. We had another trip to take. To Menlo Park, New Jersey where Mom and Dad waited for us.

"You kids need to sleep before you go," Grandpa said.

"I'm not tired," Gracie said.

"Me either," I said.

"I never got tired when I time traveled, either," Grandpa said. "No matter how long I was gone. It was as if time stood still."

Sometimes me and Gracie stay in the past for days. Then we come back home in the time machine. But our clock shows we have been gone only for a few seconds.

He closed *Little Women* and put it in my hands. "Tell Mr. Edison hello for me," he said.

I hate this part. The part where me and Gracie leave. Grandpa worries about us traveling back in time. Without him. But he can't go. He might get stuck in time too. Like our parents. Then what would happen to me and Gracie?

Gracie took his hand. "We'll be okay, Grandpa," she said. "We have to go. Mom and Dad can't come home if we don't."

Grandpa nodded. "I love you kids, you know," he said.

"We know," me and Gracie said together.

"Jinx," said Grandpa. "You both owe me a soda pop. When you get back from Menlo Park—oops!" he said.

The time machine shook again.

"Uh oh," I said.

It shivered.

"Oh no," Gracie said. She held her locket tight.

The time machine's doors flew open. A heavy wind pulled me and Gracie and Grandpa toward it.

Gracie stumbled forward. And so did I.

"Grandpa!" I yelled over the wind.

Grandpa caught hold of his desk. Then he grabbed onto my shirt. "Take Gracie's hand, George."

Gracie slid toward the time machine.

I dropped the book and reached out to her.

Little Women flew past us and inside the wardrobe.

Gracie reached out to me.

We locked hands.

The doors slammed shut.

The wind stopped.

I screamed like a girl.

Gracie raised her eyebrows. "You screamed," she said, "like a girl."

"I know," I said. Because what else could I say? My whole body jiggled like jello.

"What's wrong with the time machine?" Gracie asked. She still held my hand. "It never takes us until we're ready to go."

Grandpa shook his head. "I don't know. But I think it's scared to go"—he lowered his voice—"to you-know-where." He stepped up to the wardrobe.

Gracie dropped my hand. She tiptoed behind Grandpa.

So I tiptoed behind Gracie.

Grandpa pulled on the doors. But they wouldn't open. "What's wrong?" Grandpa said out loud.

"I'm scared, that's what," I whispered.

"Not you, George," said Gracie. "He's talking to the time machine.

"Oh," I said.

Grandpa put his hand on the doors. "The kids have to go," he said. "And I'm counting on you to take care of them."

The wardrobe trembled. It said "Bl-l-rrrr." Whatever that means. It sounded like "Not in a million years" to me. Which is how I felt too.

"We'll be okay," Gracie said in a quiet voice. "No matter what happens. Me and George have each other"—she petted the doors—"and we have you. Please. Open up so we can go save our parents."

Grandpa smiled at Gracie. "Good girl," he said.

The doors cracked open.

"Yikes," I said. I hugged Gracie's arm.

"It's all right, George," Grandpa said. "Don't be afraid. You can both get in now."

Gracie climbed inside the wardrobe and sat down. Cross-legged. She picked up *Little Women*. "Are you coming, George?" she said. "We have a job to do."

That's my sister. Brave, bossy Gracie.

I climbed up next to her. Even though my legs shook like crazy.

Grandpa touched our faces. "Whatever is scaring the time machine is waiting for you in Menlo Park, New Jersey. So be aware."

The time machine quivered a little. So did my stomach.

I nodded. Gracie did too.

The time machine made a whirring sound. It lit up.

"Crowe well be there too," Grandpa said. "Watching. Waiting for his chance to grab you and the time machine. Be extra careful." He kissed my forehead and then Gracie's. "Stay together. Be safe."

The whirring sound got louder and louder. The lights flashed.

Grandpa stepped back.

We waved to him.

"Here we go, Gracie," I said.

"I know, George," she said.

Then BANG! The doors slammed shut.

And ZOOM! We were inside a black hole.

The adventure continues in

Wizard of Menlo Park, New Jersey

Coming Spring 2014 from Familius

www.familius.com

CPSIA information can be obtained at www.ICGtesting.com
Printed in the USA
BVOW02s0258290813

329755BV00002B/3/P

9 781938 301766